PENGUIN BOOKS

UNTIL EVEN THE ANGELS

Suzanne Scott Tomita was born in Tunisia and raised in Venezuela, Germany, Indonesia, Canada, and Australia. Her writing includes personal essays on the topic of motherhood, mid-life, and marriage published in Canada's national newspaper *The Globe and Mail*. She has published on the topic of home and belonging in *Expat Living* Singapore.

Suzanne has a PhD in Education from the University of British Columbia. In 2014, Suzanne completed The Writer's Studio (TWS) Creative Writing Certificate at Simon Fraser University in British Columbia, Canada, where she studied with writers Kevin Chong and Wayde Compton. At TWS she wrote the beginnings of her debut novel, a selected chapter of which is published in Emerge, SFU Publications.

Suzanne completed an advanced fiction course with author Claire Keegan in 2023 at the Asia Creative Writing Programme, a collaboration between the National Arts Council of Singapore and Nanyang Technological University. When she's not reading or writing, Suzanne walks Singapore's nature parks and visits museums imagining characters for her next novel. She lives in Singapore with her family.

ADVANCE PRAISE FOR *UNTIL EVEN THE ANGELS*

'Richly evocative and perfectly timed—Suzanne Scott Tomita propels us from the class struggles of post-colonial Singapore to modern-day London where dark truths reveal themselves amidst the fractured bonds of friends who have endured. A brilliant debut!

A mystery novel whose fragrance and intrigue linger long after the last page. A debut worthy of an Edgar.'

—Simon Rowe, author of
Mami Suzuki: Private Eye

'*Until Even the Angels* is an absorbing, twisty story of sacrifice, betrayal, and vengeance set in a 1950s Singapore that was deeply divided by race and class. Suzanne Scott Tomita deftly mixes historical incident with lush backdrops and a cast of unforgettable characters.'

—Kevin Chong,
The Double Life of Benson Yu

Until Even the Angels

Suzanne Scott Tomita

PENGUIN BOOKS

An imprint of Penguin Random House

PENGUIN BOOKS

Penguin Books is an imprint of the Penguin Random House group of companies whose addresses can be found at global.penguinrandomhouse.com

Published by Penguin Random House SEA Pte Ltd
40 Penjuru Lane, #03-12, Block 2
Singapore 609216

Penguin
Random House
SEA

First published in Penguin Books by Penguin Random House SEA 2024

ISBN 9789815204803

Typeset in Garamond by MAP Systems, Bengaluru, India

www.penguin.sg

'What the heart wants
is to follow its true passion,
to lie down with it
near the reeds beside the river
to devour it in the caves
between the desert dunes,
to sing its notes into the morning sky
until even the angels
wake up
and take notice
and look around
for their beloved.'

—'Until Even the Angels',[1]
Dorothy Walters, 2008

'He scooped and examined a handful of its body—a wisp
of bone and skin—a girl.'

—*The Good Earth*,
Pearl S. Buck, 1931

---

[1] 'Until Even the Angels' is reprinted with permission of Stephanie Marohn, literary executor for Dorothy Walters (1928–2023).

For Dr T
and in loving memory of Louisa Wawn

Prologue

You have seen me before, Detective, but you won't remember. From where I am now, on the underside of this world, I look pretty good for a half-dead woman. It was pathetic for me to be shot like this, bullet through the brain at the wheel of my own car. Indecorous, somehow.

Here, in the realm of the in between, my rage spills out of me like black seeds from a split papaya, endless like frog spawn. I raced through my free life looking for a slice of Heaven, devouring all I could, all the experiences, all the things they said I could never have. I had it all, I really did.

Now, the judges of the underworld offer me a revision of my life. This half-world bureaucracy means I take a number. I hadn't counted on the courts of Hell being so pedantic. Up ahead, a spotlight shines on a lectern holding a leather-bound book. Turns out Purgatory or wherever I am reveals pages from my past. My rage dims to a cinnamon heat. I open the book and start to read.

Part I

INVADE

Chapter One

MEI MEI

1938

George Town, Malaya

In the dark pages of the beginning there is Ling Li. She searches
the cool shadows under the piers around George Town looking
for treasures she can sell at the market. Above her, hundreds of
fishing shacks stretch out on stilts from the island of Penang for
the far reaches of the Indian Ocean. Ling Li hears the wooden
boards strain against the weight of a person and looks up. She
sees a woman kneel down and drop something into the salt water
flat. Ling Li sees it slide beneath the brown sea and follows the
ripples to pull my tiny body out of the ocean. She understands
the two reasons why I have been left to drown. One, I am a girl,
and two, the dark stain on my face places me as not just unlucky
but cursed. Ling Li cradles me to her chest and pats my back.
I choke and wheeze and cry. *I am alive.*

Ling Li staggers forward, digging a foothold in the shifting
sands. The clear current circles around her. She licks her chapped
lips, tasting the seaweed salt. I am reaching for breath. She blows
inside my mouth and my eyes flutter open. Ling Li can see they
are pale against my dark hair and light skin. She turns me over to

examine my curled back and sees a light blue-grey mark. She tries to rub it away with her thick wrinkled thumb. She needs to feed me. Maybe, later, she can sell me.

Her cousin, Su Yin, has recently had a baby, a sickly boy. Su Yin offers to nurse me, but only until another option is found. I am quiet for a couple of days, flaccid, not moving much, until one night I release an unceasing cry and the voices inside the fishing shacks threaten to quiet my screams.

'A fighter, this one,' says Su Yin.

'Let's keep her,' says Ling Li.

'Year of the Tiger,' says Su Yin. 'No one will want a wild girl.'

Together Ling Li and Su Yin care for my well-being, keep me from toppling over the edge of the pier across the bay where we make our home. The others shake their heads and say the mark on my face and my unknown parentage will only lead to bad luck, but Ling Li keeps me. She ties me to her back and calls me Mei Mei, Chinese for little sister.

A few years later, a woman from the Jesus group walks through the market and sees me squatting in front of an assortment of balls Ling Li makes out of odd rags.

'How old is this child?' asks the woman.

'Do you want to buy her?' answers Ling Li.

Ling Li moves me towards the lady and I look up.

'No! But . . . wait, let me see her eyes,' she says. 'What colour are they? Are they green, hazel, light brown with gold flecks?'

'Tiger girl,' says Ling Li.

'I can find her a home,' says the woman.

'Where she goes, I go too,' says Ling Li.

She lifts me up and wraps me in her sarong.

The woman offers Ling Li and me a small room in a house in George Town. We don't scavenge any more. The Jesus lady teaches Ling Li cleaning, laundry, and ironing. I am fed bread and biscuits I've never tasted before. I follow Ling Li copying her as she sweeps and washes the floor. The house smells of lemon and the terracotta tiles are cool as I crawl then run from room to room.

The Jesus lady gives me a picture book of a garden with people hiding behind great trees and teaches me a song about angels. She tells me about a place called Heaven where we will find Jesus, and she tells me about Hell and the Devil in the eternal fire. We live there taking in laundry and cooking until the bad war years when the Jesus lady leaves us. We are hungry all the time and stay in the house growing vegetables in the small garden. We survive, then one day the Jesus lady returns and tells us she has found us work. She knows a family we can work for in Singapore.

1949

The Colony of Singapore

My first real recollection of a past that is mine is from the grand colonial house on Mount Rosie Road. Ling Li and I find ourselves weaving in between bicycle rickshaws on Orchard Road as passengers in our new employer's car. The air cools slightly as we drive onto Clemenceau Road, past the long-gone nutmeg orchards. I see men and boys exiting a mosque, greeting each other with palms pressed to hearts. I stick out my tongue to taste the warm breeze. It is sticky and sweet.

As we turn from Chancery Lane onto Mount Rosie Road, the lush greenery grabs hold of me. Palm fronds open as if on cue, revealing tracts of frangipani trees planted purposefully to welcome visitors. The car circles to the right where a large tembusu tree with its oval green leaves and yellow flowers camouflage what looks like a swimming pool.

We follow a driveway to the left where in full view the black-and-white house is framed by a fishtail palm. It is the most beautiful house I have ever seen. Hornbills screech, then torpedo across the tops of the trees landing one by one on a tall palm, their beaks mirroring the shine of the house. Yellow black-naped orioles chase each other across the sky. A shiny black monitor lizard the size of a small dog crawls in front of the car and encircles us: I follow it with a curious sense of terror. Its tongue flickers out as it throws its claw-like arms in front of its body, a wayward front crawl. I hear the first call of the koel, the sign of the beginning and end of each day. I hear its piercing call over all the other sounds, calling, calling. The melodies are dizzying and I remember the descriptions of what the Jesus lady said about the Garden of Eden. I imagine it must have been incredibly noisy.

Ling Li tells me that I have an overactive imagination. It's true. In the make-believe version of my life at the great house, I pretend that our new employer, 'Sir', has my best interests at heart. He looks me in the eyes when I work, nodding a question in my direction, 'You all right?' he asks. *Yes, yes. I will always be perfectly fine whenever you ask me*, I want to reply. I want him to invite me close and encourage me with endless kind words. I don't see Ma'am much and when I do, I have the sense she doesn't want me here. Ling Li looks after my welfare, but she doesn't treasure me. I am a project, her investment. Even at such a young age, I sense that my place will always be about servitude unless I pay close attention and fight hard to get out.

Ling Li isn't like the other amahs who work in the wealthy homes of the Chinese and European families. Those amahs have devoted their lives to a nun-like existence of service and child-rearing. Ling Li doesn't adhere to their formal dress of dark trousers and starched-white shirts. She cuts her hair short instead of how the amahs wear a severe bun at the base of their necks. There aren't any children in the household to care for. Just me.

It is nearing the end of the Hungry Ghost Festival and Ling Li has set up fruit and cooked rice for the ghosts of the ancestors. Ling Li follows the tradition of burning joss paper as an offering to the spirits of her ancestors. We burn paper representations in a small shrine just outside our joint bedroom sending food and clothing and piles and piles of paper money to the ancestors, sending prayers into the night.

Ling Li explains to me that during the Hungry Ghost Festival the gates of Hell are opened and the spirits leave the underworld, and we have to appease them to leave us alone. She frightens me by telling me about the maze of underworld chambers where the dead must go to atone for their sins. My imagination fills in the blanks of what these places might look like when Ling Li nudges me. We lean in to hear the other servants in the kitchen house gossiping. They talk about a white girl, an *orang putih*, an *ang moh*. Maria, Maria Hertogh. Her name is whispered about in the servants' quarters, shouted about inside the grand house, and written about in the papers. Maria.

Ling Li tells me what the radio news says—after six years of being lost, feared kidnapped, Maria has been found living with a Muslim woman in Malaysia. The story is all anyone wants to talk about—how a lost girl is found, how a Dutch Christian girl is living with a Muslim Malay. I don't understand what all this can mean, but I imagine that I will meet her one day and that we will be forever friends. She will like lychees and calamansi juice just as much as I do.

Her photograph in the pages of *The Straits Times* newspaper shows a pretty girl with round cheeks, curly hair, freckles, and a sweet smile. Under the dim light in the servants' quarters, I smooth out the sheets of newsprint on the table and trace my fingers across Maria's face, linking her freckles together. Maria, the lost and found girl. I let my imagination go to her and hold it there. I wonder if after so many years away from her own family she will recognize her own mother. Will her mother recognize her own child? I feel that my heart might just burst out of my chest and bleed out all over the clean sheets I have just washed and folded. It is all too much, too much for my little heart.

It seems white mistresses is all any of us hear about these days as Sir announces to the servants that his niece is coming to live at the house. I wonder about this girl, Miss Honour Hamilton. I imagine that she will look just like sweet Maria. I picture us entrusting one another with secrets, playing games, and looking out for one another's best interests. The other servants, the Tamil maid, Vee, and the Muslim driver, Suleiman, all of us are curious.

'What will I prepare for her to eat, will she eat European food?' asks Cook out loud.

'What will she do all day, will she go to school?' asks Vee.

'Just more work for me to do,' says Ling Li.

'Another child,' says Vee.

'Mei Mei, come! Make extra room extra clean!' Ling Li says.

'Why?' I ask.

'Don't ask, just do. Must make everything clean,' Ling Li insists.

'Why?' I ask.

'The young mistress. She coming here, to live, about your age,' says Vee.

From the top of the main staircase, which, as a house girl, I clean but never use, I see a skinny child step out of the car. I can't see her face, but I sense a sadness about her, the colour of asphalt. This girl is nothing like I imagine Maria to be. Nothing. From where I am standing, I see her long, tangled brown hair with a crooked velvet bow, her arms hang without purpose beside her. Ma'am Tessa never embraces Honour. Angus Sir reaches for the girl and I am struck by the urgency with which the girl's arms wrap around his waist and the envy that grabs my heart. My envy has a colour, the colour of tripe before it is boiled: greenish brown.

An old woman the servants call Aunt Faith lumbers out of the car and walks slowly up the steps behind Honour. She rubs her hip as she walks tenderly towards Ma'am. Aunt Faith is broad around the middle and seems to be wearing too many layers for the humid weather. Ling Li comes up behind me on the landing of the stairs.

'Watch out for that old woman,' she tells me. 'She can understand Hokkien, Malay, *and* Mandarin. Make sure now that you never say anything bad about her, she understands everything. She grew up in this house.'

My eyes widen at the thought of this old woman as a young girl like me.

'Tessa! Tessa, my darling, you do look well and you too Angus,' says Aunt Faith.

She kisses them on both their cheeks and continues to speak as she moves deeper into the house.

'How are the servants? How's the young gardener working out?'

I hear the old woman's voice echo in the heart of the house with no pause for response. She rattles on about the state of the gardens, how uneven the road has become, the difficulty of retaining good servants, the insincerity of Sir's business partners. She has a vested interest in Sir's business affairs. Ling Li tells me that Aunt Faith's grandfather founded a rubber plantation in Malaya over a hundred years ago and the family lived here. In my eyes, Aunt Faith reminds me of the Jesus lady. She is strong and watching, always watching.

Ling Li summons me to unpack Honour's clothes. Honour is lying upside down on the bed in her room: her stringy hair drags on the ground. Her mouth moves where her eyes should be and her chin has become her nose. It is unnerving and I am wary. She sits up slowly, tracking me with her blue-black eyes following my movements as I work to unpack her trunk. I feel her staring at the mark on my face with pity and disgust. She moves in front of her mirror and holds up a dress. I am unaccustomed to being with other children and my gaze explores everything about her.

'Go away!' Honour growls without looking at me.

I understand this sound. It is a warning. 'Back up, go back.' But something in me stirs. She isn't Ma'am, or Sir, she is just another child like me. I walk backwards towards the door and as Honour moves to close it, I keep my fingers curved around the doorframe just a bit too long, daring her to harm me. She watches as I walk down the hall to the steep back staircase to the kitchen house, my chin jutting out purposefully: my full lips close around my crooked teeth. That girl, that oily-haired, upside-down girl is to be my new mistress.

I work hard every day. On mornings when the sun is strong, I air dry the washing. Sometimes I can smell the ocean on top of the hot winds, bringing me faint memories of the sea at George Town. When the rains lash the sides of the kitchen house, the corrugated iron roof peels off the covered walkway connecting the grand house to the servants' quarters and flies out over the grass. On those days, when the winds are fierce, I retreat inside the room I share with Ling Li, and feel the burden of my work adding up.

The new clothes dryer often breaks down and the clothes stay wet and stink and I have to rewash. Ma'am wants everything crisp, white, and tight. Bright and starched. To get the washing to her liking, I map out stains; from mouths, privates, stains of sickness, from every orifice of the people at the house and work at removing any signs of imperfection. But with my wild imagination, I can predict what's ahead, disease, heartbreak, and loneliness. I can predict loneliness, my own loneliness.

Chapter Two

DETECTIVE AYESHA NUR

12 November 1999

City of Westminster, London

Detective Ayesha Nur leans in through the shattered window of the luxury Mercedes sedan, her London Metropolitan Police–issued flak jacket presses against her chest and she coughs into the fog. The rain has stopped, but it is cold. She shines her torch over the figure slumped across the passenger seat and inhales quickly. Broken glass sparkles like diamonds all around the woman whose manicured hands are folded together as if in prayer. The front dashboard is covered in blood, the smell of hot metal hits Ayesha in the back of her throat. The radio is still playing: classical piano, a counterpoint to the car alarm. Ayesha takes off her glove and checks for a pulse. She sees the woman's fingers twitch.

'Victim alive! Life support!' she shouts.

Ayesha takes note of the severely injured woman. She is well groomed. Her luxury accessories show expensive if not ostentatious taste. A red snakeskin Louis Vuitton purse; her watch a gold Cartier Panthère. There is even a hint of the new Givenchy perfume in the car. The woman looks to be Asian and in her early sixties with jet-black hair. Detective Ayesha Nur has seen her share of gang assassinations, but this investigation is her first to lead. The situation disturbs her in a way she can't comprehend. Not yet.

The London Ambulance Service arrives. Attendants file out and load the severely injured woman feet first through the back doors. The blue lights from the van brighten the walls of the apartment buildings on St James's Place.

Inside the police vehicle, Ayesha pulls up the integrated homicide investigation report on the police laptop. The vehicle is licensed to a Charlie Xioa. His photograph fills up the screen and the hair on her forearms stand up. She recognizes this face. Ayesha's partner, Police Constable Steve Chua, folds himself into the driver's side of the car next to her. Steve is lanky and young with boundless energy. He rubs his large hands together.

'It's like Siberia out there tonight,' says Steve.

He pulls the jacket of his collar up towards his chin.

'Another triad assassination gone wrong?' asks Steve.

'No idea yet,' says Ayesha. 'Found any ID?'

'Voilà! Her wallet,' says Steve.

He hands the wallet to Ayesha. His hands bump against the steering wheel and he drops it on the floor of the vehicle.

'Who is she?' asks Ayesha.

'Hang on, let me reach for it . . . She is a Ms Isabelle Goh,' says Steve in a theatrical manner. 'Madame Goh, someone sure didn't like you very much. Think she'll make it, Chief?' asks Steve.

'Doubtful,' says Ayesha.

Ayesha types in 'Isabelle Goh'. Alerts with tabs labelled 'loan shark' and 'human trafficker' pop up immediately.

'Does that say Interpol?' asks Steve. 'She's wanted by British and Singaporean police?'

Ayesha scrolls through the reports stating that an Isabelle Goh, also known as 'Mei Mei'—the ubiquitous Chinese term for little sister—is wanted for extortion, loan sharking, even human trafficking. She reads on. Graphic images show a burned down home, a family trapped inside, charred to the bone. A photograph of a man gunned down on the steps of his Putney home, his pre-teenage daughter lying beside him with her throat slit. There are images of young women with beaten faces outside a maid agency in Singapore. But to Ayesha, the most upsetting report is the one filed last Sunday claiming that Isabelle Goh used children as human shields.

A photo of Isabelle running out the side door of the children's market in Covent Garden holding a young boy out in front of her causes Ayesha to place both hands over her mouth.

'You see this? Last Sunday, at Covent Garden,' says Steve. 'What kind of animal . . .'

'God, how did I not . . .' says Ayesha.

'What's wrong?' Steve asks.

'Oh my God,' Ayesha says.

She knows these people.

'What? Chief? You all right?' asks Steve.

Ayesha begins to remember. She recalls where she has seen Charlie Xiao's familiar eyes, the shape of his forehead, Isabelle's pixie face and crooked mouth. Her daughter, Zoe, was at their grandson's birthday party, the one where they rented the entire Convent Garden children's market.

'I can't do this,' she says.

'What? Why not?' asks Steve.

'You know why,' she tells him.

'Kids?' asks Steve.

'You know I . . .' she begins.

'. . . can't cope when kids are involved?' asks Steve.

'Correct,' she says.

'It's just your average gang murder, you've got this. I know you can do this,' says Steve.

Ayesha clenches her jaw, straightens her shoulders, and takes in a heavy breath.

'You're right. I *can* do this. I just . . .' she says.

Ayesha looks through the woman's wallet and finds a photograph worn at the edges. She looks closely and sees a sepia-toned image of three children. Two girls and one boy. The girls, one Asian, one Caucasian, look around age twelve. The boy looks older. His head is thrown back in laughter. The Caucasian girl wears a velvet bow askew on her head, her arm is thrown around the Asian girl's shoulders, possessively. Their cheeks are pressed so close to each other, it is as if Ayesha can feel their warmth.

'Steve, this is hard for me,' she says.

'You can do this, boss,' says Steve.

Ayesha reaches into her jacket pocket and squeezes the felt heart Zoe made for her on Mother's Day. Deep down in her body's memory is the desire to search for Zoe's hand and never let it go. She has a colour for this love; a swirl of dusty rose and robin egg blue.

Steve and Ayesha head to the address on the driver's licence. Steve forces open the front door of Isabelle Goh's St James's Place flat. Forensics will be there later. Steve stays on the ground floor while Ayesha takes the stairs and heads for the second-floor landing. The master bedroom faces Green Park. Inside the large, opulent room, she finds a massive TV, luxurious animal furs. Around a corner is a walk-in closet. She turns on the lights to reveal a room just for handbags, luxury purses. Ayesha sees the newest Goyard bag, over two thousand pounds. Then there is Gucci, Chanel, Alexander McQueen. 'Pay attention to the clues,' she tells herself.

Ayesha looks for accoutrements of the gangster lifestyle, links to casinos, bags of cash, a safe where Isabelle would keep her documents, passports. Ayesha works with a wired focus to look for clues, any details that show a pattern of criminality, but everything is carefully put away, very tidy and clean.

She walks back into the bedroom and over to the dressing table when something catches her eye. Ayesha sees a photograph stuck into the mirror frame. She takes it off and looks at it up close—a young Asian girl, a Caucasian girl, and a slightly older boy, South Asian. The same children as in the photo in Isabelle's wallet. Behind the children she sees a Christmas tree framed by tropical plants. She turns it around anxiously. Someone has written in ink—Christmas, 1949. Her first real clue. It is a high she is addicted to. Her curiosity is paying off.

'Chief?' Steve calls her from downstairs. 'We've got a live one.'

They aren't alone. *Shit*, thinks Ayesha. She rushes to the master bedroom door, calling for reinforcements on her radio.

'She's unarmed,' says Steve.

Her back against the wall, Ayesha steadies herself and walks slowly down the stairs. Steve is at the bottom holding a young woman by the shoulders. Her hair is matted and hangs in front of her face.

'She's injured. Badly,' says Steve.

Ayesha sees a petite woman holding a blood-soaked towel around her arm.

'Found her hiding under the kitchen sink,' says Steve.

The woman stumbles forward. Ayesha can see this woman has lost a lot of blood.

'Have forensics check for ID and fingerprint the place,' says Ayesha.

'On it, boss!' says Steve.

'We're taking you to the hospital now,' she tells the woman.

Ayesha and Steve rush her to the police car where the woman sinks into the back seat. Ayesha can smell a strong medicinal scent like tiger balm emanating from the woman.

'Can you tell me what happened?' asks Ayesha.

The woman shakes her head and squeezes her eyes shut, breathing rapidly.

'Steve, gun it! We're going to lose her,' says Ayesha.

Steve turns on the sirens and races to the A & E at Charing Cross Hospital.

Detective Ayesha Nur is familiar with emergency rooms, personally familiar. Not that anyone would know. Her history with them is private. It started even before her daughter, Zoe, was born. She couldn't shake the increasing intrusive thoughts: the house wasn't clean enough despite her endlessly scouring corners with bleach and cleansers. When she got pregnant, Ayesha felt compelled to rid the house of all small objects that the baby could choke on, before Zoe was even born. Ayesha obsessed over the quality of the tap water. She even had a Thames Water Utilities' inspector come to the apartment to test the plumbing. None of these things had ever entered her mind before. And when Zoe came early, Ayesha couldn't shake the feeling that something was wrong with her baby. Ayesha insisted the hospital conduct scans and endless tests. Zoe was small but otherwise a perfectly healthy baby.

Then, after nine days, Ayesha just couldn't get out of bed and lay in her bedroom staring at the ceiling. She blamed herself for the baby being early and no matter what the doctors and nurses told her, Ayesha couldn't change her thought process towards her natural strengths of logic and reasoning. She locked on depression and guilt and started to unravel. Valve by valve she felt her heart shut down so that it felt like only the minimum amount of blood was keeping her alive. Everything stopped. Her hair stopped growing, her fingernails stunted, she felt her heart collapse into itself leaving her static and empty. She didn't dream for a whole year and rarely spoke during her maternity leave.

Gradually the horror of her postpartum depression stopped playing in a continuous loop. The sadness is still there, like the feeling of being upside down in her own head, looking out onto the world as if she is a sole actor on a stage, but Ayesha manages her anxiety. Medication helps, but she worries that the contours of her heart can close at any time and that she won't be capable of loving Zoe.

Ayesha and Steve enter the automatic doors of the A & E holding up the injured woman.

'Ah, the alluring aroma of vomit and warm piss! A & E *numero cinq*,' Steve says in a mock French accent.

The emergency is busy with people smoking while pushing IV poles. Other patients lie still on stretchers in hallways, like an army of fallen soldiers. People are swearing, scratching pus-filled scars, and open wounds. Steve finds a wheelchair. The woman collapses into it. The three of them make their way to the admissions nurse.

'Under investigation, any private rooms?' asks Ayesha.

The admissions nurse laughs.

'That's hilarious. Private room? Busy night for you two,' she smirks.

She has blue tinged hair and sucks on an oversized Scotch mint. A male nurse with a sleeve of ornate Asian-themed tattoos stands beside the admissions desk. He is pushing an IV pole. His name tag says 'RORY'.

'Come on then, let's take a look at your injury. What's your name, love?' asks the admissions nurse.

'Mariflores,' answers the woman in a whisper.

'That's a pretty name,' says the admissions nurse. 'My name's Dawn, can you tell me what happened?'

Rory moves towards Mariflores to examine her arm.

'No, don't!' Mariflores flinches away from his touch.

'It's all right,' says Dawn.

'No!' screams Mariflores. She keeps her mouth open in a silent scream and Ayesha notices the upper row of gold teeth in the woman's mouth.

'You're all right,' says Rory.

'No! Get me away from here!' screams Mariflores and bashes her arm against the side of the wheelchair.

'There, there, come now, steady,' says Dawn.

'No!' Mariflores pants like a wild animal.

Rory approaches Mariflores and holds her steady as Dawn unwraps the bloody towels from Mariflores' hand. Mariflores winces, the bottom half of her fingers are partially severed, most of the flesh, bone, and tissue lie fragmented inside the towel.

Mariflores grunts and bares her gold teeth at Dawn and Rory.

'Get away!' Mariflores screams.

Mariflores starts to shake. She starts to speak quietly to herself and starts to cry. Blood seeps onto the floor.

'Blood—STAT!' calls Dawn.

'On it,' says Rory.

Mariflores raises her voice and starts yelling in a language none of the nursing staff can understand.

'Call a code white! Bring her to Bay C and call Dr H,' says Dawn.

Mariflores is extremely distressed and flings her head backwards, her mouth agape, and screams, 'No, no,' over and over as she is moved inside the ward. Steve follows Rory as he pushes Mariflores into the emergency room. Ayesha stays with Dawn to complete the admission. Dawn looks at Ayesha in all seriousness.

'Believe it or not, I've seen this before. No way this was an accident. Looks like . . . torture. Is this why you're here? My God. You did good bringing her directly here, and after we attend to this injury, she'll need Dr H in psychiatry . . .' says Dawn.

'Dr H?' asks Ayesha.

'You must be new. Never heard of Dr H? Seen it all,' says Dawn.

'And the other woman, brought in overnight, with gunshot wounds?' asks Ayesha. 'Did she make it? I'll need to interview her.'

'In ICU. She'll be there a long while yet. Miracle she even made it,' says Dawn.

'When will I be able to interview . . .?' asks Ayesha.

'Let us do our job first, Detective, we'll let you know,' says Dawn.

'Right, and this Dr H? Where can we find him?' asks Ayesha.

'She's over in ABSU—Acute Behavioural Stabilization Unit. Down the hall beside the security booth,' says Dawn.

'Right,' says Ayesha. 'Thanks.'

'New investigative team, very green,' mumbles Dawn to herself.

Ayesha wonders how this hospital building is still standing. Fibre optic cables and ancient plumbing thread and rethread the historic hospital walls crawling up and down like obscene vines. It will be some time before Ayesha and Steve interview any of the victims.

'So, Chief. What connects the two? Isabelle and Mariflores?' asks Steve.

'Hmm?' Ayesha is thinking.

'The two women—how are they connected, then, what does your spider sense tell ya?' asks Steve.

'Evidence before intuition, Steve, you know that,' says Ayesha.

'Yeah, but it's pretty obvious. Mariflores was in the wrong place at the wrong time. She saw something, or whoever tried to take our Ms Goh threatened Mariflores too? Triad?' Steve asks.

'Way too risky to be in central London with all the CCTV . . .' says Ayesha.

A voice over the loudspeaker strains. 'Code white, Weston Ward 5 CD—code white, Weston Ward 5 CD.'

'Shall we go find this Dr H then, eh?' asks Steve.

Ayesha looks through the glass panel of the lock-down unit. It is full. Ayesha's new to the Central London circuit and hasn't met the psychiatry team yet, but she does remember hearing about this Dr H, how she is known for her expertise in managing extremely challenging cases in forensic psychiatry.

'Code white, Check: Weston Ward 5 CD—code white, Weston Ward 5 CD,' the voice over the loudspeaker repeats the code.

'Violent patient, that is,' says the young security guard inside the booth cocking his head towards Ayesha.

Thanks, Captain Obvious.

'Hi, ya,' says Ayesha.

'What you investigating, then?' asks the guard.

'A couple of cases, it's been a busy night,' says Ayesha.

'Always is around here,' he says.

'So, what's Dr H like then, eh?' she asks him.

'Dr H? She's incredible. I'm scared of the people here, man,' says the guard.

'Does she work every day?' asks Ayesha.

'No, only shift work here, Detective—no attachments that way,' says the guard.

'I get it,' she says.

'You'll need to bring your A game with Dr H . . . don't get on her bad side. Like, ever. I've seen her be ruthless one minute and an angel another,' says the guard.

'Good tip, thanks,' says Ayesha.

'Hear that? That click, click, click sound? That's her. There she is! Always in heels,' says the security guard, nodding in the direction of an older Caucasian woman. 'Oh, and she has zero time for the police. It's patients first every time.'

Dr H is elegantly dressed. With her chestnut brown bob and pearl earrings, she looks like she belongs on the cover of *Town and Country* magazine not here in the A & E. She exits the ABSU unit and makes her way deliberately to the emergency area. Ayesha walks quickly after her.

'Detective Ayesha Nur. Do you have a moment?' she asks.

Dr H walks on down the hall without stopping to acknowledge Ayesha. Dr H looks intently down at her clipboard.

'No,' says Dr H.

'I need your expertise, your assistance in a case . . .' says Ayesha.

'I'm in the middle of my work day, as you can see,' says Dr H.

'As am I, Doctor,' says Ayesha.

Dr H stops still and looks up from her clipboard.

'Yes, well, what is it?' she asks.

'I'm leading a case. A patient . . . multiple bullet wounds . . .' begins Ayesha.

'It's been busy,' says Dr H.

'We believe we have a witness, here in emergency, she's lost a lot of blood, in severe shock, a psychotic break, perhaps . . .' says Ayesha.

'I heard the code, Detective,' says Dr H.

'This patient, she's our prime witness,' says Ayesha.

'Patient well-being is my priority, Detective,' she says.

'I've already had calls from the media asking if it's a triad, assassination . . .' begins Ayesha.

'Detective, your emergency is not my emergency,' she says.

'The thing is—' says Ayesha.

'Excuse me, please,' says Dr H as she begins to walk down the hall.

Ayesha follows Dr H through the crowded hospital corridor.

'Doctor, we have reason to believe others are potentially at risk. Other women and children. I need to know when I can interview both women, Isabelle Goh and Mariflores,' says Ayesha.

Dr H stops and removes her eye glasses, then places them on the top of her head. She looks at Ayesha and shakes her head.

'The media. Did you say the media have contacted the police?' asks Dr H.

'Yes, they are speculating the woman is involved in a triad, but no triad would conduct their business here in the centre of London. CCTV cameras everywhere. And the target of an assassination attempt is rarely a woman,' says Ayesha.

Dr H puts her glasses on again and rests her hand on the DSM IV bulging out of the front pocket of her white coat.

'Not my area of concern. I shouldn't be speaking with you,' says Dr H.

'And another thing, the woman's injury is to the hand, the admissions nurse says this is a pattern, she's seen a similar injury . . .' says Ayesha.

Ayesha notices for the first time that Dr H is wearing a tan coloured leather glove on her left hand.

'Is that so?' says Dr H.

'Yes, what would this mean?' asks Ayesha.

'No clue,' responds Dr H.

Ayesha pulls her flak jacket down towards her hips. The pager attached to Dr H's pocket starts to beep and she tilts it towards her line of vision to read.

'Where is the patient, Detective?' she asks.

'Emergency Bay C,' says Ayesha.

'If you're asking for my expert opinion, I would say this is a warning,' says Dr H.

Dr H swipes her ID to unlock the doors into the A & E and they hear Mariflores screaming right away. The phlebotomist is administering O negative blood as well as pain medication through an intravenous. Mariflores looks terrified.

'I have to go back, lah! No. I must go,' screams Mariflores. 'I didn't steal! Let me go.'

She is writhing on a gurney and continues to bang her injured arm against the bed frame. Rory, the male nurse, holds her down. Dr H steps towards Mariflores and puts a hand on the woman's shoulder.

'You are unwell, Mariflores, we need to give you some medication to calm you down,' says Dr H in a kind voice.

'This patient requires twenty-four-hour supervision. Place her in ABSU. Give Haldol 5 IV!' says Dr H firmly to Rory.

'No, I will be killed if I stay, I must go, now,' whimpers Mariflores. 'Help me! Why won't anyone help me?'

'We are helping you,' says Dr H calmly.

'Who is going to kill you?' asks Ayesha.

'Detective, I can't have you here,' says Dr H.

'I need to leave. Please!' pleads Mariflores.

'We will help you, but we need to ask you some questions first,' says Ayesha. 'Why don't you tell me what happened?'

'Detective, now is not the time,' says Dr H.

Rory and another nurse wheel Mariflores, on her stretcher, out of emergency and down the hall towards ABSU. Ayesha follows Dr H through the locked doors of the specialized unit.

'Detective, once again, please let us calm the patient,' says Dr H.

'Doctor, Haldol administered,' says Rory.

Ayesha stands outside the unit and waits to be readmitted. She knows from experience that twenty minutes should do the trick and bring calm to the distress. After half an hour, Rory opens the doors and nods to Ayesha.

'You may have a brief conversation with my patient,' says Dr H.

Ayesha sits on a stool and moves it close to Mariflores.

'Mariflores, hello. I'm Detective Nur, here to help you. Can you tell me what happened?' asks Ayesha.

'I fell. I tripped, the food processor cut me,' says Mariflores in a small voice.

Before the medication, Mariflores looked like a trapped animal lashing out for survival. Now, she appears peaceful.

'What were you making?' asks Ayesha.

'Huh?' Mariflores is confused.

'What were you cooking when you fell—you said you fell?' asks Ayesha.

'Detective, that's enough now,' says Dr H.

'Cooking. No, no cooking,' says Mariflores.

'Where did you fall, in your house?' asks Ayesha.

'Not my house,' says Mariflores.

'Whose house do you live in?' asks Ayesha.

'Ma'am's house,' says Mariflores.

'What ma'am? What is her name?' asks Ayesha.

'I don't know name, I only know Ma'am,' says Mariflores.

Ayesha watches as Dr H takes complete control of the environment, administering medication and placing restraints, all while keeping her tone calm.

'You are safe here. Your job is to heal,' says Dr H.

Dr H's pager goes off again. She reads the message and beckons Ayesha to follow her to the corridor.

'We need to keep her under observation, she'll need the antipsychotics to really start working before we get the plastics consult, she'll likely need some fingers amputated,' says Dr H. 'You need to let us do our job.'

'But—' says Ayesha.

'Leave Mariflores here with us. Try the other patient, seems there's been a miracle in the ICU. Isabelle Goh, she is responsive. Third floor, Ward B,' says Dr H.

Detective Ayesha Nur runs up the stairs two at a time.

Chapter Three

ISABELLE GOH

13 November 1999

London

I sense the room around me. It is warm. An oxygen mask has been placed over my nose and mouth. I reach for my face and pull it off. I've never liked enclosed spaces and I need air. I am unsure where I am. I last remember sitting in my car. After that, I remember nothing, but strangely my past is clear. I can recall faces from my time as a girl at the great house. There is Ling Li, the Jesus lady, Maria. I can see Honour, Vee, Pash, and Rosie, my Rosie. I close my eyes and can conjure up these people from my childhood.

When I open my eyes, I can make out someone is in the room with me. A woman in a police uniform stands at the foot of my bed. I want to sit up and ask her what she's doing in here with me, but I fall back into a fog of exhaustion. Hours later, I wake up and the woman is still standing there.

'Leave me alone,' I say.

'I can't, I can't leave you alone. You are a victim of an attempted homicide,' says the woman.

'Do you know who I am?' I ask.

'Your ID says Isabelle Goh,' says the woman.

'Correct. Yes. I was the most successful—' I say.

'London's most successful estate agent . . . isn't that what your advertisements say? Until, your life was almost taken from you,' says the woman. 'You are lucky to be alive, the shots were close range . . .'

'They tell me a bullet is wedged close to the brain stem,' I say, licking my dry lips.

'That is correct,' says the woman.

'I'm on a pretty tight timeline then,' I say.

'You could say that,' says the woman.

'And you, officer, what is your role in all of this?' I ask.

'Detective Ayesha Nur, I'm leading the investigation,' says the officer.

'Very young, you seem, very young to me,' I tell her and start to cough.

'You've made some serious mistakes. I'm sure you have a few enemies. We have a guard posted outside your room twenty-four hours,' she says.

I draw in breath and cough again, spluttering.

'Tell me, Detective, what do you know about . . . the world, about how it works, really works?' I ask.

'I understand it to have its highs and lows,' she says.

'And betrayal, what do *you* know of betrayal, Detective?' I ask her.

'We've all had our own share, I suppose.'

'Yes. Correct,' I say.

The pain is starting. I can feel the morphine starting to subside. It feels like a sharp pickaxe tapping gently against the side of my temple.

'Can you tell me who would want to do this to you, Isabelle?' Detective asks.

'I can imagine quite a few people actually,' I say.

'And betrayal, what do you know of it?'

'I know it intimately.'

'I'm all ears. I'm here to interview you.'

'You want my whole story?' I ask.

'Where do you want to start?' she says.

'With the cracking open of my childhood, the heartache of lost friendship, you know, the usual,' I say.

'Ah, a simple way to begin,' says Detective.

'I guess I will have to start with Honour,' I say.

'Honour?' she asks.

'Yes, Honour, it all starts with Honour and the house . . . the house on Mount Rosie Road,' I say.

I close my eyes and slip back into the shadows. I feel myself dipping into the underworld again and feel the gun wedged against my temple. And suddenly, everything is clear. I, Isabelle Goh, know what my heart wants. It wants Honour and Rosie and Maria. It wants for us to be together one last time.

'Here is what I remember, Detective. An account of my life. Make yourself comfortable.' I begin.

I was just a poor, illiterate girl working as a maid servant. I would have had an unremarkable life, except that my life intercepted with Honour's. Meeting her made me desire a future I never imagined could be mine.

All of us are in servitude, Detective. Mind you, just with different masters. In the days when Ling Li and I were captive in our fear of the Kempeitai, of bombs, of our own hunger, the Jesus lady told me to look for Heaven. She told me to look for it here, here on earth, in the dark green of the pandan leaves, the bright yellow feathers of the orioles, in the smell of frangipani, and the gentle touch of a cool breeze before a thunderstorm.

Ling Li and I lived in the small house in George Town hiding from the war, growing kitchen greens to not starve to death, and the next thing we knew, we were domestic servants working in the most beautiful house in all of Singapore. Despite its opulence, the black-and-white mansion had character. The white walls were fixed in place by black timber frames around large windows and doors. Bamboo chick blinds rolled up like heavy eyelids above the windows that opened out onto endless greenery. The semi-circular staircase anchored the interior of the grand house. Walking barefoot across the cool tiles, I rooted myself into this new place. Home. It was a definite improvement to the life we had in George Town, but I was still lonely, so lonely.

The Jesus lady taught me to pray and I prayed every day for friendship, for a real kindred spirit, for someone who would know me better than myself, a bosom buddy. This to me was the most precious prayer, to find another girl who would be my friend. To entertain myself, I played games encouraging my imagination to keep searching for Heaven and praying for a friend. And guess what? Jesus sent a girl, my age, but He must have a sick sense of humour. He made her my mistress. A friend in the most unlikely form.

At dusk, Ling Li lights the lanterns out in the garden for Sir and Ma'am Hamilton to enjoy in the evening. This light in the dark opens a novel dimension of time, it reflects the shadows of the palms and jungle life onto the open grass and I see a girl hovering behind the adults and want to be near her.

Vee tells me the place where Miss Honour comes from in England is cold and dark and the brightness of the tropical sun makes the girl sleepy. After one particularly long day of unrelenting heat, I see her through the doorway of the dining room. She sits alone at the big table and opens a box. I stand there with a wet rag, looking busy, when she moves her eyes over to where I am.

'Go away,' she hisses.

This seems her only refrain. But I don't budge, I hold my ground. I dare myself to go closer, to go inside the darkened room I am not supposed to enter. The furniture is too big and heavy for two little girls. I position myself beside her. I am so close I can see the severe part down the middle of her scalp and I can smell her unwashed hair.

'Do you know how to play snakes and ladders?' she asks.

So many words all at once. Her voice is desperate. I nod although I don't understand her question.

'Mei Mei,' I say pointing at myself.

'Honour,' she says. 'Sit.'

She starts talking to me, more talking at me.

'Roll the dice, like this,' she says and rolls a three.

I pick up the dice and roll a straight six. She smirks, then moves our tokens—first hers three squares, then mine six squares. When it is my turn again, I roll a second straight six. She sits up straighter in her chair, like she knows she has to pay attention now. She seems impressed.

'My turn,' she says.

She rolls and lands on a snake and reverses her token back to the start.

'You're just lucky,' she says.

I reach for the dice. I see Vee pass by the doorway and smile.

'No, game finished,' Honour says.

I look at her blankly. Vee nods my way, encouraging me to stay fast and keep playing.

'Game finished?' I ask.

'It is,' she says. 'Does it hurt?' she asks, pointing at my face.

'No,' I respond.

'Looks painful. Can't you rub it off?' she asks.

'No,' I say and look away.

'Can you read?' she asks.

'Yes, no read,' I say.

I can't read. It is another thing I long for. Friendship, and reading.

'How old are you?' she asks.

I hook the heels of my feet on the back rung of the dining room chair and shrug.

'You don't even know how old you are?' she asks. 'Well, I'm eleven,' she says.

She holds up both her index fingers, each white finger standing straight out.

'Eleven,' I repeat.

She rolls her eyes and shakes her head.

'Twelve next week,' she says.

I nod and smile.

'Useless,' she mumbles. 'I'm getting new coloured pencils for my birthday and Uncle has promised me more paper.'

She takes her colouring pencils out of her craft box. The sheets of drawing paper are lumpy from the moisture.

'Can you at least draw?' she asks. 'You know, like this?'

She starts to outline a flower with big loopy petals and a thick stalk. I pick up one of the coloured pencils and reach for a piece of paper.

'Good God!' she says.

She grabs the pencil crayon from my hand and holds it in her fingers.

'Hold it like this, not like that!' she says.

She draws a house and a girl.

'Here,' she turns the page towards me.

'HOUSE, GIRL,' she says and labels them with letters and hands the page to me. Then she snatches the page back and adds the word STUPID beside the word GIRL and laughs, flicking her dank hair off her shoulder.

It turns out the feng shui master we visit is right. Ling Li and I meet with him at the start of the Hungry Ghost Festival and he tells us what he always does: We should save our money, work hard, and burn Hell banknotes for our ancestors; but then, quietly, under his breath, he says that a new person is coming to the house and will bring trouble.

'New person, bring trouble, ah,' he clicks his teeth together and shakes his head. 'Can't be helped.'

'What you mean, Uncle?' asks Ling Li.

'Energy wrong. Energy all wrong, lah,' he says.

He has a square head and a thick neck. The pockmarks high up on his cheekbones give him an air of danger, an edge, like he has seen battle and walked through fire. I keep my fingers from wanting to touch the small scars on his face that look like the air bubbles in the prata that Cook makes on Saturdays. The feng shui master has an extra thumb on his right hand. I imagine him as half crab, half man scurrying across the floor after our visits.

His eyes carry a light behind them that can see far beyond what we can. He rolls out long sheets of paper with tiny etchings on them. Ling Li leans in closer to the feng shui master, holding the collar of her blouse closed. I know she doesn't want him to see her new gold chain bumping against her chest or the new butterfly tattoo she doesn't think I see on her shoulder.

'Mei Mei will have trouble, not good,' he says.

'What can be done?' asks Ling Li.

'Nothing. Nothing can be done,' he says.

'Always something, Uncle, something can be done?' she asks.

'Cannot help if Mei Mei no birth date. Only trouble,' he says.

'Mei Mei, she is good, she works hard,' Ling Li shares.

'Yes, but no birth date, no future. *And* she is a Tiger girl. The stain on her face, unlucky, no parents, nobody knows, nobody wants,' he says. 'Everything out of balance, no good, ah.'

As he tells us this, he shifts his position on the stool, clears his throat and rearranges the sheets of charts. He addresses me directly.

'Mei Mei, there is one thing you *can* do,' he says.

'What, tell me, Uncle? Win the chap ji kee? Find a real tiger? I know, find Heaven? I'm sure I can, I know I can,' I say.

He laughs and rubs the top of my head. I can feel the nub of this extra digit rub against my scalp. As he pulls back his hand, his fingernails get caught in my hair.

'Don't ever lose your imagination, ah!' he says.

'Can't lose. It's a part of me,' I say.

He looks around as if making sure no one else can hear him.

'Good,' he says. 'Know who you are. Carry it in your heart.'

Later, back at the house, I ask Ling Li what the feng shui master means, no future. Ling Li laughs awkwardly and lights an extra joss paper. We send a new paper car, clothes, and coins to the underworld. We spend our hard-earned money on appeasing the dead and in turn ask for protection. The ancestors are not poor.

'Pay no mind. I'll make sure you have enough,' says Ling Li.

Despite Ling Li's reassurances, I am disturbed by the prophecy. I cuddle with my doll that night, the one Ling Li gifted to me from the Jesus lady's market. I pull my doll close, pat her chest. I wait for Ling Li to sit on the edge of my cot to let me know everything will be all right, but she never does.

That night I fall asleep watching Ling Li counting the banknotes she keeps under her flimsy mattresses while the paper money, the ones we offer at our shrine, burn up in flakes of ashy smoke. What the feng shui uncle and Ling Li don't know is that I am *not* good. I lie. I have my own money, money from another source. From Ma'am. Ma'am pays me to keep her secrets. I look out to ensure her privacy. I fold the banknotes Ma'am gives me into tiny squares and feed them down the open hole at the back of my doll's throat. My money is safe and sound inside the belly of my doll.

Chapter Four

ISABELLE GOH

1999

London

The surgeon has removed four out of the five bullets. One is lodged in my brain stem, bullet in bone, never to come out. The fact that one bullet remains makes me furious, as if the surgeon is making a point. *Not going to let you forget, you don't have much time.* I *am* running out of time, but I have so much to tell you, Detective. Just promise me this one thing: You will find Rosie.

You keep asking me about Mariflores, but to be frank, it could have been any number of women who got in the way, casualties to the real crime. It's all part of the way I learned to operate. I am an expert at finding people to put in between me and real danger.

At the great house, not much joy came my way and a childhood was not something I ever had. But I did have my imagination and this quest to find a place called Heaven, the place where the Jesus lady told me we will all go if we live a good life. And so, to quell my loneliness, I imagined Heaven everywhere I went: in the teakwood trees, the lipstick palms, the flowering bougainvillea. I saw Heaven in the swirls of coconut milk in my bowl of laksa, in the yellow centres of the frangipani blossoms, but, I never did see Heaven in people, until Rosie. But we'll get to her.

The first time I see Ma'am with another man that isn't Sir, I am home alone. Cook is sick and Suleiman has taken him with Ling Li to see a doctor. Vee is visiting her sister and Sir is down at the port. Ling Li tells me Sir oversees the shipping business that Aunt Faith's family set up years ago with Mr Lim from the well-known Peranakan family.

Mr Lim is in the study with Ma'am. I am outside in the stone courtyard chasing the sun to dry a pair of Ma'am's shoes, when I look in the bay windows. Ma'am is bent over a chair. Mr Lim stands behind her. Her yellow skirt balloons out over his chest, like oversized petals opening up and out to him. The chair moves across the floor as his weight pushes the chair forwards until he folds himself onto her back. He stretches out his chin, arches his neck and shudders. I turn away and run to the servants' quarters overturning a bucket of water on the flagstones. My heart is racing. I am not sure that what I have seen is pleasure or pain or love or hate. I empty soapy water into the drains that run alongside the walkway and feel sick. Later that day, Ling Li calls me to buff the skid marks off the wooden floor in Sir's study. I never see Ma'am again with Mr Lim, but it is not long before she finds another man.

At the house, I observe Honour and copy everything she does. I watch how she styles her hair and start to wear a clip across my forehead the way Honour does. I cut a piece of the soap from her bathroom and use it so I can smell like her.

During Honour's swim lessons, I stand in the shade and watch from the base of the garden. I move my arms up and back like she does, practising the same strokes. The oval-shaped golden light sparkles across the water, then light rain starts, and soon after comes down with a power so strong each rain drop seems to reverse its direction. I watch the torrential rain.

The rains keep Honour and me inside. We sit across from each other on the back steps under the veranda. Honour tells me she is beginning to like the food Cook makes. She says she prefers noodles, dumplings, and mango now over English food.

During these wet days, moving back and forth between the house and the servants' quarters, I imagine that I am journeying between foreign lands. The foods and languages are completely different. My behaviour changes. I need to stay small and quiet in the main house, whereas travelling the other way, back to the kitchen house, I am welcomed with a smile from Vee and a cock of the head from Cook. I always feel bigger and more myself upon returning to where we servants live.

Keeping clothes washed and dry is an unending task. As I walk in the kitchen house carrying a basket full of dirty clothes, Honour is still sitting on the back steps. The clouds are starting to clear.

'Want to trade? You know, you give me your doll, I'll give you whatever you want,' she asks.

I nod, feeling warm inside. I have something she could possibly want.

'So, what do you want? You know, of mine,' she asks.

'Keep teaching me,' I say without thinking.

'Fair trade,' she says.

Honour continues to teach me to read. She holds up pictures of an apple, a bird, a cat, a feather until I can put together the images, letters, and sounds. B.I.R.D. I follow the letters and say

'BIRD'. Then, as if on cue, the koel pierces the dusk with its high-pitched cry. I know there is a nest nearby. Ling Li says the koel birds are parasites, they trick other birds to bring up their own eggs, then push the host birds' eggs out of the nest so that the nesting bird only has the koel's eggs to nurture.

'Parasite,' I say the word out loud and wonder how to spell it.

I keep matching images and letters and sounds until a pattern emerges. I search for words throughout the house to read: on Sir's album covers, I read the words 'sea pictures' and in Ma'am's women's magazines, the words 'how to keep him happy'. I am collecting words to teach myself how to make sense of Honour's world.

The second time I see Ma'am with a different man, it is a beautiful morning. Pillars of giant white clouds are mounted across the blue sky. The steady breeze dries the washing quickly. On top of the warm wind, I am alerted to a foreign smell, a sharp, unpleasant sweetness, like heat against the back of my tongue. I follow the smell, checking the dryness of the laundry framing the back garden and part the sheets hanging behind the kitchen house and hear groaning. I haven't heard that sound before, and then I hear Ma'am's moaning.

Before I move past the last bedsheet, I have a feeling deep in my belly—of unease, of danger, of something a child should not know, and then I see them. Ma'am is sitting on top of a man. Her yellow skirt is fanned out framing the act. She eases her hips sideways and back and forth holding on to the grass in front of her. Her hair hangs down. The man's face is covered by a sheet. A dried line of red mud coats the edges of his shoes. I gasp loud enough for Ma'am to look up.

'Mei Mei!' she calls out.

I run. I run to the edge of the jungle to get away from her and that man. I pace beside the vegetation, touching the ferns to calm myself. I know I am in trouble somehow. I don't know what I saw, but it made me feel afraid and that something is wrong, very wrong.

Later that day, she comes to the servants' quarters. I am folding a mound of towels and make ready for taking them to the main house.

'Wait,' she says.

'Ma'am,' I say.

I am red in the face.

'I think you are a very brave girl, a very brave, smart girl,' she says.

I look around to make sure no one hears her or sees me. Ma'am never talks to the staff.

'I want you to watch out, to keep me private,' she says. 'You understand, don't you?'

At first, I feel special, singled-out for being resourceful, but eventually, my stomach churns whenever I see her red painted nails coiled around a damp roll of bills. She folds a thick bundle inside one of the towels I am carrying.

'Take this,' she says.

'Thank you, Ma'am,' I say.

'Good work,' she says to me as Vee walks by.

In that moment, I enter an unfair exchange. My silence for her privacy. Money for her sins. But I haven't actually agreed to anything and I don't want to be on her team. With this bribery and the others afterwards, Ma'am keeps me doing her bidding. She keeps me afraid and small. But I want to be good, I want to be big, I want to have the same opportunities Honour has. I want to be loved, to be treasured. I want to belong, to have a family.

Beyond the front gates of the house, the lane is framed by thick jungle. Massive plants emerge from the ground with shoots unfurling like tongues searching for water. Amongst the songs of birds at every register of sound, I hear frogs calling back to each other in the same timbre as dogs barking. The rustling of branches above signifies the weight of a monkey and not a jungle squirrel. Then, as the heat rises, the cicadas, the army of sounds, lift me up like a buzz of energy and carry me through my tasks until the inevitable rain quells the sounds.

Amongst sweeping frangipani blossoms and dry leaves at the front gates one afternoon is where I find myself when I am up against that smell again of the man with the mud on the rim of his shoes. Zandstra's profile reminds me of a sucked mango pit—the top of his unkept head is uneven like orange pith. I stop sweeping as he walks past and step back into the jungle. He never notices me. His scent hangs in the air as its own cloud, like I can walk in and around it. It is menacing: It smells like anger and power and danger. I follow this scent like a dog to the front of the house.

Zandstra stands on the front steps of the black and white. He lights a cigarette. The same ones I sweep up. I stay near the porte-cochère watering some of the planters. I reach for the ridges of the new leaves coaxing a new tendril, urging its erect buds to look for the sun. His smell lingers. I close my eyes and breathe in not because I like the smell but to teach myself, to warn myself what danger smells like—sickly sweet with a hint of heat.

I move back into the shade and squat in the grass, pocketing the red saga seeds. From where I observe him, Zandstra is watching Pashunath, Vee's nephew. We call him Pash. When I look back, Detective, Pash was really beautiful; beautiful Pash. He didn't know his own beauty.

Pash is standing on a ladder, reaching for stray branches. Zandstra blows out his cigarette smoke in the direction of Pash. I can see that Zandstra admires Pash's back, his side muscles, his long legs.

'Boy, come down!' says Zandstra.

'Sir?' says Pash.

Pash climbs down and wraps his lungi closer around his hips and pulls his white singlet up over an exposed nipple.

'Come closer,' says Zandstra.

Zandstra strokes his goatee, taking in the length of Pash's torso.

'Sir,' says Pash.

'Closer, closer,' says Zandstra.

'Yes,' says Pash.

'Don't be afraid,' says Zandstra. 'You, boy, you like working here?'

'Yes, Sir,' says Pash.

'So, what flowers does Ma'am like, then, eh?' asks Zandstra.

'Sir, I . . .' says Pash.

'I asked you, what flowers does Ma'am like, boy, tell me!' demands Zandstra.

His short temper comes from nowhere and seems to heat the already hot air.

'Zandstra!' calls Ma'am from the front doors. 'You're not leaving, are you? Come inside, let me pour you a drink.'

Her sing-song call brings Zandstra inside and away from Pash. I memorize his menacing smell. There is something else in his scent I can't quite place, then I find it. The missing ingredient from Zandstra's dangerous smell is sweetness edging over into excess. The same smell from the glasses I clean when Sir has his men in his office after dinner. Ling Li tells me the drink is called whiskey. The word sounds whimsical, like a whistle, but the smell is something different, and combined with Zandstra's name, it makes me feel sick. Zandstra is an angry sound, like an outdoor garden chair being dragged across flagstones.

Chapter Five

DETECTIVE AYESHA NUR

September 1999

London

When Zoe started at her new school, Ayesha remembered feeling awkward around the other parents. At the social held for the new families at Zoe's posh new school, Ayesha made an effort to chit-chat with the 'yummy mummies'—the women with social and real capital. Ayesha had neither. She and Dom had split two years ago and with his earnings from his real estate dealings, he had insisted on paying for Zoe to have an expensive education. The whole independent school scene was foreign to Ayesha, but she wanted the best for Zoe.

Ayesha made conversation with some of the other mothers about after-school activities and the teachers, but her eye was drawn to a man wearing a brightly coloured jacket. In the living room of the Chair of the School Board, this man stuck out. Ayesha's police training had prepared her to look for patterns that didn't fit the norm. There was an older grandmother at the event who also didn't seem to fit the pattern of the other affluent parents, but come to think of it, neither did Ayesha. She never seemed to fit in anywhere.

As the man circled the guests, she watched his body language go from controlled gentleman to gangster bodyguard. She noticed how, when he followed the grandmother about the room, his shoulders buckled forward, on his guard like a panther. In that instance, Ayesha could tell that they were playing pretend, rubbing shoulders with the well-heeled school families. Their attempt to infiltrate this crowd was leaving them exposed. What did the woman say her name was again? Oh yes, Isabelle.

Ayesha was born Ayesha Yuet Lin Nur to a Chinese mother and Malay father. Her parents had immigrated to the UK from Malaysia and had made their home in Leeds where her father drove taxi. Ayesha remembered the thrill of reading old Nancy Drew novels her father would bring home for her from the free box at the library. Her reading room was the inside of her father's taxicab along the streets in Leeds where the winters were dark and wet. Ayesha grew up in that taxicab, one of the few servicing the region. She would retreat into her crime novels and follow the mystery as clues unfolded.

Her father would pick up a drunk from the Legion swearing racial slurs or a woman fleeing domestic violence or a person coming back home from the clinic, clutching bad test results. Her father listened to old cassette tapes of Malay folk songs, the songs of his heritage, the subtle tabla drums lulling her to sleep in the cozy taxicab, the feeling of his warm palm against her forehead keeping her safe.

One night, when Ayesha was twelve, she was an innocent victim of gang violence. She had been waiting for her father to pick her up from track and field practice when a random gunshot hit her left leg, tearing her muscle and requiring emergency repair. Gang violence. She had wondered what that term meant and now she was working at the centre of it. Through her school days, she was self-conscious of her scar, but she kept running and was a member of the track and field team at Kent. Later, after completing her degree in Criminology, she worked as a frontline London constable. She saw her fair share of addiction, violence, and domestic abuse. This new post as detective with the London Metropolitan Police was right where she wanted to be.

Chapter Six

ISABELLE GOH

1999

London

We have met, Detective. It was at the school social, don't you remember? It was where, for a brief moment, I felt like I was on top of the world. I had constructed Isabelle Goh, matriarch, successful businesswoman, grandmother. I was rubbing shoulders with well-heeled Londoners. Not serving them. I'd succeeded in duping the school to admit my own 'grandson', all in exchange for an introduction to the new market of wealthy Asian families wanting a British education for their children. I have always been good at exchange. Exchange of loyalty has been my currency for most of my life until, I have to admit, my luck began to run out.

You asked me if my grandchild was happy at school. I took a sip of the cold wine, pulsing the liquid over my tongue, holding it just below the roof of my mouth, tickling myself from the inside. I let go of the constant wariness of watching out for my life.

'Yes,' I said, 'very.'

I felt you could tell I was lying and that I really had no idea. No idea about my so-called grandson's welfare.

'Your . . . child?' I asked you back.

'She has her ups and downs,' you replied.

'Who is your grandchild?' you asked me.

Charlie walked over towards me at that moment and I turned to reach for a second glass. I excused myself feigning a phone call I had to make. I had a sense you knew about me and about the identities I was hiding. I saw in you an equal, someone who would understand the things I have done, the ways in which I have been made to serve to survive.

Chapter Seven

MEI MEI

1949

Singapore

I can always tell who is home by what is on the radio. Ma'am listens to the news, Sir to classical music. When the news is on, we servants learn more about Maria, the lost-and-found girl. At first, the English words on the radio are muddled, but soon I start to form letters in my mind. One minute they are the colour of charcoal that Cook uses to make satay, then as voices are pointed, the words ignite in my mind to a burnt orange. We hear that Maria and the woman who took her, Che Aminah, will come to Singapore for meetings at the court house.

'That poor girl, taken to court,' says Vee one evening.

'How you mean?' asks Ling Li.

'The mother wants the girl back after all this time, but the girl don't even know her own family,' says Vee. 'So sad, I wish I remember my mother. I know this to be true, that girl just needs love.'

Vee's words are the perfect temperature, warm and soft.

I don't like it, but I can tell Cook and Ling Li make fun of Vee. They mock her food. They say the smell of her curries and spices is too strong for the other servants, and these dishes are not what they prefer to eat. Vee knows they tolerate it when she cooks. I find myself attracted to her customs. My shared room with Ling Li is filled with orange and red. Our little shrine works overtime, dedicating prayers to the ancestors. The incense is high on the nose and makes me sneeze. In Vee's room, she keeps a small shrine where she burns incense that smells earthy, with notes of cinnamon and cloves. This is where she prays for the good health of her sister and Pash.

I walk past Vee's room and see that her door is slightly open. The top of her chest of drawers is lined with purple and green silk. Jasmine and marigolds strung on long garlands hang around a small mirror. When Vee sees me, she reaches out. She smells like coconut.

'Mei Mei, you need some comfort, come girl. How are the games with Miss Hamilton?' she asks.

'She always wins,' I say.

Vee laughs and I can see the back of her tongue. It is white with orange stains. Her body shakes when she laughs, and I am amazed at the vastness of her bosom.

'Oh yes, she will always win,' laughs Vee knowingly.

'How so?' I ask shrugging.

'Let her win,' says Vee. 'Must always let them win.'

'But . . .' I begin.

'I know, I know, hard for you, lah, you are a strong one, our Tiger girl, but must, must always let Miss Honour win, ah,' she says.

Vee zips open a colourful bag full of creams and cosmetics. She applies a coconut-scented lotion across her forearms.

'What about Pash, you say to him same thing?' I ask.

'You've met my nephew, Pash?' she asks.

'I see him some days,' I say and catch myself blushing.

'Why you blushing girl? You think he's handsome?' asks Vee. 'That he is. Come, come closer, let me put cream on your face, let me see!'

Vee starts to add tinted cream over the stain on my face.

'Oh, Pash so lucky you know. Sir, so generous, he pay for Pash,' she says.

'For what?' I ask.

'For learning. Sir pays for his learning. He study at St Andrew's, one of the finest boys' schools in Singapore,' she says in a lilting voice.

'So Pash is winning,' I say.

'Pash knows, he knows he needs to be on same side, same side as Sir. Listen to me, no good to talk like this. Just be grateful, lah,' says Vee.

'Grateful,' I repeat.

'You know, Pash had to leave school during the war. Pash older than other boys, but so smart, lah. I'm glad Pash can have future, good future,' says Vee tugging an apron tight around her waist.

She holds her hand mirror up to my face.

'Look! You could be a real beauty with those eyes!' says Vee.

I look into my reflection and I am amazed. The stain is almost gone. I look like a totally different person. The skin on my face is smooth and hides the mismatch between the two sides of my smile.

'There, you look beautiful!' says Vee.

I laugh into my palm and blush again. Vee continues, her voice full of pride.

'Sir, he teach Pash to learn. Sir, he borrow Pash books and records,' says Vee.

'Pash lucky, lah,' I say. 'No school for me.'

I turn from her and look again at my face. Where my Tiger eyes a minute ago flashed light, now they have turned black. I understand the playbook now. I am just a girl, a girl to be used. But Pash, Pash is seen as a worthy investment. Sir pays for Pash to gain knowledge while Ma'am pays me to keep her secrets.

Honour and I build a fort in the eaves between the two roofs of the kitchen house walkway and Sir's study. We drag palm husks and large leaves and bring them up to our fort, building a secret nest just for the two of us. From here, we have a perfect view of most of the activity in the house.

One Sunday afternoon, Honour and I play hide and seek. I've never had this feeling before: the anticipation of being found, of hearing a countdown before the hunt. The forced silence, the excitement of hiding, all of it has a beautiful colour, and this time I sense a texture—the paper-thin, fuchsia bougainvillea leaves we hold between our fingers. To me, this is the feeling of waiting for the moment to be found. I love this feeling.

Honour races up to our secret spot where she finds me hiding. We are both out of breath.

'Found you!' she yells. 'Good spot!' she says and knocks me over with a shove.

'Again!' I say. 'Let's play again.'

'Wait. Shh. Look!' she says pointing down at the walled garden as we slow our breaths.

From our fort, we stand together. I am so close to her that her tightly woven braids give me a sympathetic dull ache. I follow her outstretched arm down into the walled garden. Along one wall is a solitary faucet where Pash begins and ends his gardening day. Kneeling down in front of the faucet, we watch as Pash scoops up the water and rubs up behind his ears, his thumbs leading the way. His skin is the colour of the table in the dining room. He breathes into his hands and sighs as the cool water soothes his face. He splashes the water up over his mouth, nose, and eyes and then back again with more sighs.

He finishes washing, dries his torso, hooks his lungi up over his hips, circles his arms, and loosens his shoulders. His walk is deliberately slow: a straight walk miming bowling a cricket ball. Again, he retraces his steps and mimes another bowl and silently cheers when he hits the wicket. I see flickers of white where his palms turn to me. These repetitive movements and sounds, the strength of his broad hands, are to me the ultimate power. I want to be strong like Pash and clever like Honour.

'I like him,' says Honour, giggling.

I feel a stirring of darkness that surprises me and the joy of our game disappears. *No*, I tell myself, *he's mine*. I am surprised by my own thinking.

Pash has a bicycle that he uses to come to work on Sundays at the great house. I see it leaning against the stone wall and although it is too large for me, I pull it and walk it slowly in a circle. I am curious about it and wish to learn how to ride.

'You like my bicycle?' asks Pash. 'Come,' and he picks me up and places me on the seat and walks me around in a widening arc.

'I like, let's go fast,' I tell him.

'Move up then!' he says.

He straddles the bicycle and puts me on top of the handle bars. He pushes his foot off the ground and we start to move. First towards the front of the house, then down the long laneway. I feel like I'm flying. The wind in my hair makes me feel like I'm free and I loosen my grasp on the handle bars. I can't help but scream with glee. Pash laughs as I relish this feeling. When we turn around and head back up towards the front of the house, Honour is standing with her hands on her hips.

'My turn!' she says pointing at the bicycle.

A week later, when my chores are over, I wait for Honour behind the kitchen house and see her running across the grass singing, 'I'm dreaming of a white Christmas.' I have brought her my doll. We play tag and run across the wide-open garden. Honour picks up as many frangipani blossoms as she can and throws them up above our heads.

'Look! It's snowing!' she laughs.

'Snowing!' I copy her voice and laugh.

She holds my doll above her head and we spin around and around. The dark timber beams and whitewashed walls of the house fly around our heads and we both fall down laughing. We get up and move on towards the back of the garden, following the chant of the Imam's call to prayer. His voice climbs high from the minaret of the mosque behind the house calling all believers. The song reaches out to us, up and over the wall. *Allahu Akbar. God is most great.* We hum along with the voice on the loud speaker and hop over the stone path collecting our bounty of sweet, sticky flowers. Honour cradles them carefully in her arms.

Pash is up ahead putting away his gardening tools inside the shed near the garage. He sees us carrying our bundles of frangipani blossoms. He joins our silly game and laughing, the three of us continue throwing them up above all of our heads, collecting and throwing them up as we all move towards the garage.

The garage door is open and I move inside ahead of Pash and Honour. I try to stop Honour as she runs in, but it is all too late. The three of us are thrown into a scene as witnesses to a union we wish we had never seen: Zandstra, the man with the muddy shoes, with Ma'am. Ma'am's face is open, Zandstra's mouth is on one of her breasts, his fingers on the other. His lower body is moving on top of hers, her skirt is drawn up over her hips. Ma'am moves her head towards the door and sees us. She pulls frantically at her blouse, bringing it down over her exposed breasts and pushes Zandstra off herself. She is screaming my name.

'Mei Mei!'

I turn and run, dropping my doll, leaving Honour and Pash, a bouquet of frangipani spilling onto the ground; Ma'am Tessa's open jaw and Zandstra's red muddy boots forever seared in my memory. I am in big trouble now.

The next day, delivery trucks bring ice and champagne to the house for the Hamiltons' annual Christmas party. The gardens are being decorated with ferns and red ribbons. Cook, Vee, and Ling Li are busy preparing food as a group of singers practise their carols in the living room, their voices filling the house with a human chorus I have never heard before.

Sir has called all the staff to receive a gift from him. He is seated in front of the Christmas tree, I am uncertain as to why a tree is inside the house but love it. A photographer calls Pash over to stand with Honour and me and takes our photo. He makes us laugh by pulling faces and I cover my face with my hand. Sir gives me a present wrapped in shiny gold tissue and I close my eyes wanting to remember this feeling forever. This feeling of laughter, of song, of belonging, and the smell of good food.

'Go on then, unwrap it,' says Sir.

I unwrap the gift. It is a shiny gold chain with a cross pendant.

'Thank you, Sir,' I say.

'Thank Ma'am, it was her idea,' says Sir.

I can't manage to look either of them in the eye, so I turn and run back to the kitchen house clutching the necklace in my sweaty hand. I hold it so tightly, the cross leaves an imprint on my palm.

Ma'am comes into Honour's room that night before the guests arrive. Through the gap in the door, I see Ma'am lean in towards Honour's mirror and draw a pencil line around her lips, filling them in with her signature coral colour then pressing them together repeatedly.

Her pale skin is flushed, her blue eyes look bloodshot. She's wearing a silver dress with gold sleeves. She sits on Honour's bed and pulls her blonde hair off her neck and up into a French twist. Removing the bobby pins she is holding between her teeth, she inserts them one by one along the curl of the roll and inspects her handiwork. I am in the bathroom cleaning up and can hear the conversation.

'I know what you saw yesterday, Honour, but you mustn't tell Uncle Angus or anyone about it,' says Ma'am. 'I was just helping our neighbour, Mr Zandstra, feel better. You understand, don't you?'

I can see the back of Honour's head. Honour nods.

'Grand. Oh, and don't listen to that girl Mei Mei, she's all lies. Stupid girl, left this in the garage,' she says.

She throws my doll at Honour. Honour sits on the bed, not moving. After Ma'am leaves, I move quickly down the backstairs to the kitchen house. She is waiting for me at the bottom.

'You, you bad, bad girl. You forgot to watch in the garage, now you've gotten yourself into trouble. It's time to stand guard, Mei Mei, and don't you dare mess up this time,' she hisses.

That night, after I've listened again to her grunting, and Mr Zandstra's groaning, I take out the children's Bible the Jesus lady gave me. I look at the detailed drawings of locusts and a man's head chopped off on a platter, of floods, men with manes of hair tearing down walls, and I can't sleep.

The games Honour and I play after what we saw are not right. We just copy what the adults did. One game does leave a scar. We are in Honour's bathroom, sliding down the back of the tub when Honour injures her tailbone on the faucet. There is a small, clean tear in her skin and a stream of blood trails in the cloudy bathwater. She holds onto her injury while tears well up in her eyes and she locks in a scream. I help her back into her clothes and put my shift dress on. I dutifully clean the bathtub, my fingers knowing where to turn the cloth around the porcelain curves, brushing down towards the drain, removing the evidence of our games. Honour is left with a bruise, but on my heart is a scar.

A week later, I sit under the giant fishtail palm, feeling the space between the jungle and garden. I smell the earth. I touch my favourite palm, a fan palm. My index finger coaxes the studded veins under each ruffled leaf. Honour squats nearby and reaches for the touch-me-not plants whose delicate leaves fold in on each other as if hiding a secret mid-tale. I sit opposite her, touching a patch of the creeping plant.

'Live or die?' she asks, more like demands.

I shake my head. 'No, I don't understand.'

'It's a shame plant, if you touch it and it folds away, you die,' she says and pushes me over onto my back.

She straddles my chest and starts to tickle me. I start to laugh.

'Die, die,' she calls out laughing as she tickles me more.

I can't help myself. I laugh and laugh and then lose my breath, starting to choke. She holds me down, her knees on top of my elbows.

'Die!' she calls out, lunging more of her weight onto my chest.

I am desperate for breath. She spreads my arms out wide and I can't catch my breath. I try to say the words 'No!' I worry I won't breathe again as I watch her thin hair fall out of her braids and her teeth start to grind.

'Please,' I manage to wheeze out.

'Die!' she laughs.

Then her weight is off me. I have a profound feeling of relief. It is Pash. He stands over both of us.

'Okay, ah?' he asks us both.

I am embarrassed and roll over onto my side to breathe and choke.

'What do you want?' she demands.

'Checking everyone okay,' he says softly and walks away back to his gardening duties.

I shed tears of shame and confusion. I realize there is a desperation in Honour, an unpredictability, a rage about her, and that it will aid me to keep Pash close.

Back in the shared bathroom in the servants' quarters that night, I prepare for bed. I copy Pash's movements, scooping water over my face. Water splashes on my neck and dribbles down my arms. I recall how Pash's muscles along the side of his torso grew taut. I wonder what he thinks of as he cools his body down when I hear someone behind me. Honour is reaching out to touch my face.

'Go away!' I say.

Her words thrown back at her. She races out along the covered walkway and back up to the main house. This time I tell her off. We are even now.

Chapter Eight

MEI MEI

1950

Singapore

Pash is finishing up gardening late one Sunday. He is washing out a pail with a hose when Honour walks past. He sprays her feet. I see them tease each other. I am hesitant and a bit wary of Honour, but I want to play too. Ma'am calls me from inside the living room.

'Tell Cook I am out for dinner, just Sir and Honour tonight,' says Ma'am.

'Yes, Ma'am,' I say and open up the patio doors to the darkening night. I stay and listen to Sir and Ma'am talk, drawing the linen drapes away from catching on the door frames.

'This business with the Hertogh girl is not looking good,' says Ma'am moving out onto the patio.

'Not our business, really,' says Sir.

'It's dreadful, there must be something we can do, you know, for the family,' says Ma'am.

'Best we leave it to the courts,' says Sir.

He gets up and lights a cigarette, blowing his smoke out towards the open veranda. I stay still in the shadows, fingering the silky smooth curtain tassels.

'A child's future is at stake,' says Ma'am.

'Since when has any child's future been your concern?' asks Sir. He shakes his hand to extinguish the match.

'A bit harsh, Angus, really,' says Ma'am.

'Right,' says Sir. 'You can't stand Honour and you treat Mei Mei abysmally.'

'Neither of them is my problem,' she says.

Ma'am tosses her hair back and pours herself another drink. Sir sighs and brings his hand together in a fist and walks to the veranda. He sees Pash act out bowling a cricket ball, the elongated arc of his throw, the exaggerated run, skip, and curl. Sir calls out towards the expanse of green grass.

'Know how to bowl, Pash?' asks Sir.

'Sir? Yes, Sir,' says Pash.

'Come on then, let's have a go,' says Sir.

I can see Pash's smile. His eyes light up with recognition.

'Got a ball?' asks Sir.

Pash produces a ball and holds it high.

'Yes, Sir!' says Pash.

Ling Li circles the patio lighting the lanterns. The garden glows gold.

'Come on then, let's have a game, there's a bat here somewhere,' says Sir. 'Let's see you take your best shot then! Come on, Honour, Pash.'

It's Pash. Pash who is brought into the family circle. Pash, not me. I move back inside and go to the porte-cochère to pick up some stray branches. Ma'am is standing there waiting for me. She hands me a roll of bills as she gets into her friend's car.

'For next time,' she says.

Chapter Nine

ISABELLE GOH

1999

London

At such a young age, Detective, I learn how humans use each other, how some of us are valued and cherished and others cast away and forgotten.

I walk towards my room, past the shrine Ling Li tends to. Piles of newspapers are folded beside it. The front pages show the face of Maria, the lost-and-found girl. I bring the paper closer and try to make sense of the letters and words, but I can't. I crunch up the papers and throw them on the floor. I head into my room, reach for my doll, and shove the money Ma'am gave me down my doll's throat. It is getting stuffed.

I imagine the day when I will be a Ma'am. I will not have to do any more work. I will have my own room with matching bed covers, pillows, and sheets, all in lavender, and a chair just for sitting in. No work. I lean back on my bed and hold my doll. She feels heavy and soft, like how I imagine a real baby feels. She has a puckered mouth and black hair sprouting out in all directions. I hold the doll against my chest, angle its head onto my neck and pat its back.

'You're a good girl, a good girl,' I murmur over and over.

I cuddle my make-believe baby, soothing myself with a gentleness not offered by anyone. I imagine having my own child one day, a girl. This sense of knowing that I will be a mother is a secret within me, a love I secretly nurture. One day, I will give myself over to it. But for now, I am complacent, compliant. I do what Ma'am wants.

But oh, Detective, how my soul aches for me as a child. I just needed attention and kindness, nothing more. Perhaps my future would have turned out differently if I had been shown some love. My little heart could have woven itself into fibres of kindness, but with each banknote my heart started to calcify into a hard, stenosed pump.

Chapter Ten

DETECTIVE AYESHA NUR

1999

London

Ayesha's depression and anxiety keep her vulnerable to feeling overwhelmed whenever children are involved. She needs to be strong, to not give herself over to her self-doubt, to her self-hatred. She manages to stay stoic and strong, suppressing her fear or emotions of any kind. It's easier for her that way. She leaned on Steve, her partner, for anything to do with children.

They have access to Tom, the boy Isabelle Goh claims as her grandson. They are interviewing him for more information about this woman lying in the guarded hospital room. Ayesha sees that Tom has a small head and a sweet face. Steve moves his chair closer to Tom in the interview room and Ayesha watches as Tom twitches. He moves away as if Steve is going to hit him.

'It's okay, buddy. Tom, I'm Constable Chua, you can call me Steve.'

Tom nods.

'Is it okay if I ask you a few questions?'

Tom shrugs.

'We need you to help us find out about your grandmother. Do you think you can do that?'

'Yes,' says Tom.

'So, tell me about her, your granny,' asks Steve.

Tom's feet swing back and forth under the grey bucket seat. 'She gives me presents,' he says. His is a sweet, soft voice. He holds a small race car in his hands: a silver Mercedes. 'It's just like her real car and it goes really fast,' he continues. Tom comes alive and jumps out of his seat. He races the car with electric energy up and down the carpet.

'That is a very nice present. Could you please sit back in the chair? Would you like something to drink?' asks Steve.

'A Coke,' says Tom and smiles.

Ayesha is shocked at how decayed Tom's teeth are. They are black and framed with silver wiring as if the last ditch orthodontic efforts are ever going to be able to salvage the rotten teeth.

'Tom, do you remember when she gave the car to you?' asks Steve.

'I have a room full of cars. She gives one to me every time I stand guard,' he replies.

'Oh, very brave, where do you stand guard?'

'At home. Most of the time she is still sleeping. I have a chair and I sit outside her door and wait for her to wake up.'

'When is that?'

Tom shrugs.

'You are very brave to stand guard. Who are you guarding her against?' asks Steve.

'Yes, I have to be extra brave,' says Tom.

'Where are your Mum, your Dad?' asks Steve.

'Gone,' says Tom.

'Who gives you your meals, a bath?' Ayesha asks Tom.

'Mariflores, she always gives me my favourite foods. Fried chicken and pizza,' says Tom.

Ayesha and Steve swallow hard.

'Mariflores? Where is she now?' asks Steve.

Tom looks away and furrows his brow. He slumps his head and shrugs.

'What about Charlie?' asks Steve.

Tom returns to playing with his toy car. He races it back and forth across the interview table.

'Charlie?' asks Tom.

'Does he help you?' asks Steve.

Tom laughs.

'No, no, that's silly, he's mostly in China. He's been there a long time, since my birthday,' says Tom.

'And when's that?' asks Steve.

'I was born on Christmas. Granny calls me her Christmas baby,' says Tom.

'Lucky you,' says Steve.

'Not really, birthdays at Christmas mean waiting all year for two sets of presents, not great,' says Tom.

'I would agree. How about at your house, does anyone visit you, at your house?' asks Steve.

'People come at night. I hear them sometimes.'

'Who are these people?'

'I don't know. They like to play games with my grandma.'

'What kind of games?'

'Dunno, I think something like . . . I'm not sure.'

'Anyone different come to the house, like, in the last few days?'

'Yes, one lady came, but my grandmother never wanted to talk to her. A lady doctor.'

'What did the lady look like?'

Jesus, thinks Ayesha, it can't be but worth a shot. Steve brings up a photo of Dr H on his laptop.

'Tom, I have a photo of a lady here, is this the lady you said came to your house?' asks Steve.

'Yes, that's her. The lady doctor,' says Tom.

Ayesha takes a sharp breath, feeling the sense of excitement before the chase.

'Thank you, Tom,' says Steve. 'You have been very brave. I'll be right back.'

Ayesha and Steve exit the interview room.

'This is it, bring the good doctor in for questioning,' Ayesha.

The November fog wraps around the city streets. It's like London is covering up a story, keeping its secrets hidden. But Ayesha is laser focused now and determined to understand how and why Isabelle and Dr H are connected.

Ayesha and Steve sit in an interrogation room waiting for Dr H to arrive for her interview. She is late.

'Didn't peg Dr H as tardy,' says Steve.

'She'll be here,' says Ayesha.

Steve raises his eyebrows and starts to make a joke about the calm before the storm when they hear the telltale click-clack of Dr H's high heels.

'Apologies, I know, I don't like to be late, it goes against my very nature . . .' says Dr H shaking out a wet hooded poncho.

'Thank you for coming,' says Ayesha.

'I was waylaid by a colleague of yours, a Commissioner Archer, Charlotte Archer?' says Dr H.

'Archer?' asks Ayesha.

'Please take a seat,' says Steve.

'I was called in to speak with the Commissioner about the case right before this meeting. Apparently, she told me there's no reason to pursue any further investigation, I'm only here to let you know, I'll not be staying,' says Dr H.

'I'm not sure I understand, *I* am leading the case, Dr H,' says Ayesha.

'I must have misunderstood then, although this woman, Archer, she seemed pretty clear that there was no need to pursue . . .' says Dr H.

'How is Mariflores? How is your patient, Doctor?' asks Steve.

'She's much better, still in the ward, but doing much better,' says Dr H.

'And Isabelle, do you think she'll pull through?' asks Ayesha.

'No,' says Dr H. 'She might hang in there for a week or two max.'

'This is a complicated case, and getting more so, it seems,' says Ayesha. 'Do you know why anyone would want her dead?'

'We all have a past,' says Dr H. 'What are you getting at, Detective?'

Ayesha's phone rings. She excuses herself and takes the call outside the interview room, in the hall.

'Nur, cease all interviews,' says Detective Commissioner Charlotte Archer.

'Commissioner?' asks Ayesha.

'You heard me. Your involvement is no longer needed. Nothing further to investigate here. Case closed as far as you are concerned. We'll take it from here,' says Archer.

'But . . .' says Ayesha.

'Drop it, Nur,' says Archer.

'I don't understand,' says Ayesha.

'You don't need to,' says Archer.

'Ma'am,' says Ayesha.

'For the last time, cease all investigation,' says Archer.

Never, says Ayesha inside her head. She is even more determined to succeed. The chase has only just begun. She will see this to the end. She may have self-doubt about being a good mother, but anything to do with her on a case, she is relentless. She re-enters the interview room.

'We have evidence we'd like to show you,' says Ayesha.

'Photographs,' says Steve.

'What photographs?' asks Dr H.

Steve pushes the image from Isabelle's wallet and the one from her mirror frame across the table towards Dr H.

'Know these kids?' Ayesha asks.

Dr H holds the photos between her fingers and looks at them closely. Ayesha watches as Dr H's eyes widen.

'Oh my, my . . .' whispers Dr H. 'She kept them, all this time.'

'Who are these children?' asks Ayesha.

'We were so young, I . . .' says Dr H.

'Doctor, who are they?' asks Ayesha.

'This is so hard,' says Dr H.

'Try, please, try,' says Ayesha.

'Mei Mei, and Pash, and me . . . Honour,' says Dr H.

'Pash?' asks Steve.

'Honour?' asks Ayesha.

'My husband . . . as a child, a young boy,' says Dr H.

'You? Doctor?' asks Ayesha.

'Yes. Me, Honour Hamilton, and Pash, Edward Roy,' says Dr H calmly. She places the photographs gently down on the table, her fingers hover over the images.

Steve and Ayesha look at each other without expressing their surprise.

'Edward. Roy . . . Bishop Edward Roy?' asks Steve.

Ayesha immediately understands why she's being taken off the case. This is major stuff.

'Yes,' says Honour.

Ayesha and Steve are alerted to the seriousness of the case, to this new turn of events, and lean in across the table.

'I was in love with him even back then. We all were. Mei Mei, me, even Zandstra in his horrible way. It was a love triangle gone bad. I never understood why Pash paid any attention to Mei Mei. But did I kill Mei Mei? No, I did not,' says Dr H.

Honour clenches her jawline and brings her hands together, interlaces her fingers, and places them on the table in front of her.

'I can't believe she kept them,' says Honour.

'Why are these photographs important?' asks Steve.

'The photographs explain the story, the reason we are together,' says Dr H.

'Please carry on,' says Steve.

'No one wanted to remember the war and after my parents died, no one really wanted to remember me, except Uncle Angus and Great Aunt Faith. I was sent off to a boarding school at age eight, but I wasn't doing well there. Aunt Faith, wisely, thought it best for me to go to Singapore with her. It wasn't until I arrived at the house that I experienced any form of kindness. There was kindness but also danger, great danger, from Zandstra, but the common denominator between everyone at the house was our love for Rosie. We all loved Rosie,' says Honour.

'Zandstra? Rosie?' asks Ayesha.

Honour's lower jaw starts to tremble.

'Who is Rosie?' asks Steve.

Honour lets out a sound of anguish, of great loss, a sound that Ayesha understands.

'Do you need a short break?' asks Ayesha.

'No,' says Honour. 'I . . . the house is where this all started. Mei Mei was mistreated by my aunt and Zandstra took advantage . . . we tried to help, we were just children ourselves.'

Ayesha observes Honour. In her state of recollection, Honour's appearance has softened from the guarded visage of a professional to a younger, more vulnerable version of herself.

'Is Rosie the reason why you went to speak to Isabelle the night before she was shot?' asks Ayesha.

'Yes,' says Honour.

'When I heard about the shooting, I was at the hospital. I assumed Mei Mei was dead. I never, ever imagined she'd live,' says Honour. She sits back in her chair and twists the bronze buttons on the cuffs of her blazer.

'It must have been quite a shock, to learn a patient is actually someone you know,' says Steve.

'Yes,' says Honour.

'Are you able to tell us more?' asks Steve.

'Last night was harrowing,' says Honour.

'That it was,' agrees Steve.

'I cycled home, after my shift. I decompress with exercise, it's the only thing that works frankly,' says Honour. 'I always pause along my favourite spot on the Hammersmith Bridge this time of year, there's a flowering honeysuckle. Have you smelled it?' she asks.

'No, I have not,' says Steve.

'Well, I love it. It smells like citrus and vanilla. The aroma takes me right back to the white frangipani blossoms I remember from when I was a girl in Singapore. Not the ones still blooming on the tree, but the smaller pink-tinged buds with the slight sour smell that lay fermenting on the stone path leading from the house on Mount Rosie Road towards the back of the garden,' says Honour.

'What made you remember your childhood, Doctor?' asks Steve.

'Seeing Mei Mei, I mean the whole situation just took me right back, that lemony sweetness pulled me right back . . . you know, the magic of dusk in the tropics, there's nothing like it,' says Honour.

'I wouldn't know,' says Steve. 'Never been.'

'There were always these tiny, white flowers on the trail behind my family's black and white. You know the scent is always strongest at night,' she says.

'Please continue,' says Steve.

'Sorry if I'm rambling, I just haven't thought of this for years,' says Honour. 'The memory is so clear. I am with Mei Mei and Pash. We follow the trail to the garage—behind it rises the mosque. I can hear the Imam's voice calling out to me up and over the wall. I'm collecting a bounty of the sweet flowers. They are so fragile; you have to cradle them carefully in your arms. We see Pash up ahead and then . . .'

'Then what, Doctor?' asks Steve, slightly impatient.

Ayesha can see Dr H returning from her memoryscape.

'I understand that all of this is a real shock for you,' says Ayesha.

'It's an old memory,' says Honour.

'Can you think of a reason why someone might want to kill Isabelle Goh?' asks Ayesha.

'What are you getting at, Detective?' asks Dr H. Her facial expression has turned serious. 'You think I tried to kill Isabelle?'

'We are still investigating, which is why we are interviewing you,' says Ayesha.

Ayesha and Steve notice Honour's hands. They are shaking.

'I can't, it's still such a shock,' says Dr H. 'It was a long time ago, a lifetime ago.'

'Please stay in London where we can contact you if required,' says Ayesha.

Ayesha opens the door to her flat, kicks off her boots, and puts on her slippers. With her police jacket still on, she reaches for her laptop and brings up the news report about Isabelle. Posts on the BBC and *The Straits Times* websites state that a notorious loan shark wanted for human trafficking is seriously injured and in hospital in London. And there it is, a quote from Commissioner Archer stating that the London Metropolitan Police, under her direction, are on top of the investigation. Ayesha is furious. She tells herself to breathe. *Steady. Focus. Focus on what you know. Don't give up.*

Ayesha hears a knock on her door. Besides Dom and her parents, she's never had anyone come to the flat since she moved in a few months ago. She turns down the lights and looks through the peephole and her heart thuds in her chest. It's Charlie Xiao. He's looking directly at her door. *Thank God Dom has Zoe all week*, she thinks. Seeing Charlie standing at her door terrifies her. Bile starts to rise in her throat and she sends Steve an urgent message.

Charlie Xiao at my door. What do I do?

Charlie continues to knock and he calls out a name.

'Zoe! Zoe!' calls Charlie.

Ayesha rushes to lock herself in the bathroom. From inside the bathroom, she hears Charlie's voice calling for Zoe and the slow knocking continues. Ayesha is reduced to a pathetic, terrified mess despite all her police training.

Coming in ten. Steve responds.

Ten long minutes, Ayesha waits for Charlie to stop calling her daughter's name, for the knocking to dissipate, for Charlie to give up.

I'm here, no sign of Charlie. Steve's texts assure Ayesha and she lets Steve into her flat.

'You okay, boss?'

'Terrified,' she says. 'And . . . confused and angry . . . he was calling Zoe's name!'

'Ayesha, there's a reason for Archer to call it, maybe it's best we let this one go, let the big guns follow up,' says Steve.

'Never! I'm certainly not giving up now,' says Ayesha.

'You sure?' asks Steve.

Ayesha is shaking but her face is focused. She nods.

'I'm in it with you then,' says Steve.

'Thanks. Please, I need you with me on the case. Can you, can you . . . stay?' asks Ayesha.

'Stay here? For the night?' asks Steve.

'Just tonight. On the settee, I can find you a blanket,' says Ayesha.

'Better than my digs, I'll stay, you go rest,' says Steve.

Later, as she prepares for bed, Ayesha hears the low throaty growl of engines and sees bright lights flickering at the back of her apartment complex. She hears male voices and parts the curtains. The back of her apartment building is swarming with men on motorbikes. They shine their headlights directly at her window, leaving her to blink back the burn behind her eyes. She sees two men standing under her window laughing. She can't be certain, but it looks like they're Charlie Xiao and Rory, the male nurse, the one with the tattoos.

Chapter Eleven

MEI MEI

1950

Singapore

On evenings when Ma'am and Sir entertain, I will myself to stay up late to see the ladies and men arrive, but Ling Li always makes me go back to our room. Honour gets to stay up and meet the guests, then she lingers at the top of the stairwell. Sometimes, Vee finds her asleep at the top of the stairs. In the mornings, I grill Honour for all the details about what the women wore, what they ate. I ask for all the specifics, filling my imagination with colours and shapes until my hunger for information is satisfied. The living room always has a different smell the next day. A hint of cigarette smoke and wine suggesting sophistication and power, which leaves me wanting more and more details about adult life.

Tonight, Honour is unsettled. What we have seen of Ma'am's behaviour has left us both confused and frightened but unable to talk about any of this. It is mixed with shame. I sneak up the back stairs into the main house after the party has started and sit next to Honour on her favourite step on the landing. I press my face against the wooden balustrades. I can see Ma'am standing below us with a group of ladies, giggling. I am holding my doll, it fits nicely in the cup of my belly: the plastic torso of the doll is cool against my skin. I tuck my nightie in around my knees.

Honour and I watch as Ma'am detaches herself from the main group of women and walks to join the man from the garage, the neighbour, Mr Zandstra, who stands directly under where Honour and I are sitting. My night dress suddenly feels too thin. I feel ill, like I have had too much ice cream. Zandstra looks up at us and touches his chest and lips, promising us that being awake late is our secret. I copy his movements, but I am tired and I lose my grip on my doll. It falls down toward the crowd of partygoers. Zandstra catches it and holds it up to us like a trophy prize he has won.

Chapter Twelve

DETECTIVE AYESHA NUR

1999

London

Ayesha wants to call Zoe, to hear her voice and be reassured that she is safe. But Ayesha knows it is best to let it go and trust that Dom 'has it'. Dom, Dominic Lee. She and Dom were a good fit at first—sexy, fun—but when Zoe came too soon and Ayesha's depression overstayed, Dom climbed further into his work life and concentrated on making millions as opposed to caring for his wife.

Dom and his brother, both estate agents, became very rich very fast, serving a steady clientele from Hong Kong and China who were buying up property in high-end neighbourhoods, bringing money into London. They could serve the Asian clientele with their working knowledge of Mandarin. But when Ayesha suspected Dom's client base dabbled in dubious investment methods, Ayesha needed off the carousel.

A week later, to allay her worry and wonder about Zoe, she heads out for her daily run. She missed her chance earlier in the day so tonight, on her run, she heads through Green Park looking up at the darkened windows of Isabelle's apartment before heading for her usual route through St James's Park. She hopes to find some respite from the rain under the dark trees. She never uses earphones. She needs to hear her own measured breath to calm her core and think. As she follows her favourite arc along the trail, her mind starts to make sense of the case. Her breathing settles and deep breaths focus her mind. *Start with what you know*, she says to herself.

She knows about the photos from Isabelle's wallet and the mirror frame. She knows that the forensics team have sourced the bullet and type of gun used in Isabelle's attempted murder. It isn't a match with any of the Asian triad work. Forensics ran fingerprint analysis, but nothing showed a connection to Asian triad violence. She knows that Isabelle Goh is wanted by international police forces for loan sharking, extortion, kidnapping, and that this woman owns an apartment in the most expensive part of London. Ayesha knows there is an injured woman named Mariflores, a man called Charlie, and a psychiatrist named Dr Honour Hamilton. *But how are they all connected*, she asks herself.

Later, back in her flat, Ayesha stretches out her legs across the coffee table, reaches for her water bottle, and takes a long gulp. An email arrives in her mailbox. It is a video link. She reviews the grainy CCTV footage of St James's Place the night of the murder attempt against Isabelle. She can make out a tall figure walk right up to Isabelle's car and get in the front passenger seat.

'Someone she knew,' whispers Ayesha. She keeps watching, and after a few minutes, the figure leaves the vehicle. Ayesha is prepared to give up, the quality of the footage is too difficult to get a sense of any features, but she keeps watching. She is surprised to find that after just a couple of minutes, a hooded figure jumps into the back seat behind the driver's seat and shoots Isabelle, five times.

Ayesha's phone rings.

'Got a moment, boss?' asks Steve.

'It never ends, does it?' says Ayesha.

'Best gig in town,' says Steve.

'What's up?' asks Ayesha.

'It's the guard on duty outside Isabelle's hospital room. He just called. Told me Charlie Xiao came to see her, the guard said Archer gave the clearance for Charlie to visit with Isabelle,' says Steve.

Ayesha feels her trust radar shift.

'Again . . . Commissioner Archer? How can they let one of the suspects in?' Ayesha blurts. 'When are we booked to interview Charlie?'

'Another hiccup . . .' begins Steve.

'What?' insists Ayesha.

'He's left the country. My buddy at Border Force called to let me know Interpol spotted him leaving London,' says Steve.

'Shite, we're not doing well here on this, what a nightmare,' says Ayesha.

'They've gone against you, sorry, boss,' says Steve.

'Double the guards at her hospital door and don't let anyone else in to visit Isabelle, I don't care if it's the Queen!' shouts Ayesha.

She is furious that her senior has allowed Charlie Xiao to see Isabelle without contacting her first and that now he's left the UK. Ayesha is anxious and when she is anxious, she can't sleep.

'I'm heading to the hospital. It'll be a long night,' Ayesha tells Steve.

When Ayesha enters Isabelle's hospital room, Isabelle is sitting up, a pair of reading glasses are on her face, and she has a magazine in her lap. There is a warm glow around her in the room. She looks like a well-meaning grandmother waiting to share story time with a group of children. Isabelle was clearly once a striking woman, with blazing eyes and an insatiable curiosity. How did this woman become a successful estate agent while hiding such a complicated past?

Ayesha approaches Isabelle's bedside. Her overcoat is folded over her arm like a protective shield. Isabelle looks up at Ayesha.

'Has anyone ever told you that your eyes, your eyes . . .?' says Ayesha.

'Tiger eyes,' responds Isabelle.

'That's it, yes! Tiger eyes.'

'I was known for my eyes. Both of us were.'

'Both of you?' asks Ayesha.

'Rosie and me,' says Isabelle. 'Same eyes.'

Ayesha moves towards the foot of the bed and sits on a stool.

'So, have you found her yet? Rosie?' asks Isabelle.

'No, I'm still trying to piece together how you knew Dr H,' says Ayesha.

'Honour?' asks Isabelle.

'Yes,' says Ayesha. 'When were you going to share the fact that you knew her?'

'Well, what's the fun in me doing all the detective work?' she mocks.

'You owe me more information,' Ayesha tells her, then gets up from the stool and moves towards the bed. 'What else have you not told me? Why was Charlie allowed to pay you personal visits?'

'I can't imagine why, but if I were to guess, probably because of the people I've helped,' says Isabelle.

'Helped? What do you mean? Define helped.'

'Exchange, I exchange secrets for other valuable information.'

'Not helping. Why was Charlie here?' demands Ayesha.

'He told me he's leaving,' says Isabelle.

'He can't leave.'

'Well, he just did.'

Ayesha runs her fingers through her long black hair, squeezing the ends. 'I need to know to be able to help you, Isabelle, and you need to start telling me about Dr H, about Honour, and Charlie!'

'I just need you to find Rosie, why can't you understand? It's that simple, all the other stuff is just noise.'

'Noise?' scoffs Ayesha.

The ward nurse arrives.

'Time for the patient to rest,' says the nurse.

'I'll be back first thing,' says Ayesha.

'Send my regards to Dom,' says Isabelle.

Ayesha grits her teeth as she pulls the hospital door closed behind her.

Chapter Thirteen

MEI MEI

1950

Singapore

I am sitting under the dim light at the kitchen house table folding linen when Ma'am walks in and asks to speak to me. I am embarrassed by her attention. The other servants leave their polishing, folding, sewing on the table and head into their shared bedrooms. I feel like my stomach is falling down to my feet. Her being here puts me at risk—at risk of the servants sensing something is off and thinking that whatever goes wrong it'll be my fault.

'Mei Mei,' says Ma'am.

'Ma'am,' I say.

'The neighbours, Mr and Mrs Zandstra, are hosting a party tonight and they need extra help,' says Ma'am. 'Come to the Zandstras' home by 8 p.m. tonight, you know the way, don't you?'

'Ma'am?' I ask.

'Right then,' says Ma'am, ignoring my hesitation.

I have never left the property unaccompanied. I mean, I've always wanted to, but not this way, not at her beck and call and to do her dirty work. When the sun sets, the whole garden landscape changes. I begin walking down the driveway to the main gate, then along the jungle road out towards Malcolm Road. There are only one or two street lamps far ahead and I walk towards them, then turn left up the hill and along the winding road past the other black and whites.

I keep walking slowly in the dark, watching out for pythons and other frightening creatures. I hear frogs and the whisking of bats above my head. I see something hopping up a tree trunk: it is a colugo. I fall backwards onto my wrists and watch as it hops and then glides from tree to tree overhead. I've only seen one once before and am alarmed by its oval eyes, too large for its head. I keep my eyes on the road ahead and eventually see the headlights of parked cars blinding my vision. The drivers lean against their assigned vehicles smoking kretek cigarettes. Then, as I adjust to the light, I hear dance music and laughter and a mixture of scents I am unfamiliar with. I am overwhelmed and tired but press forward to the back of the house in search of someone to tell me what to do when I feel nails grab the back of my shirt.

'Oh good, you're here. Time to stand guard,' says Ma'am.

I follow her up the back staircase, similarly placed as the one at the Hamilton residence. She slips into one of the upstairs bedrooms and there I keep my watch. I hear mumbling and laughter, then silence, followed by surges of grunts and sighs. I am in the dark.

The thing about people like me is if we keep being pushed down, we don't disappear, we dig into this darkness and make it our new home.

Another day and another visit from Zandstra. I have come to recognize his scent from greater and greater distances. I am carrying a load of soiled napkins and tablecloths from the recent luncheon when his familiar odour hits me. Today, Zandstra smells like the purple fluid that leaks from the car exhaust pipe and slithers on the ground like an oiled snake that, at any minute, can turn into a dangerous gas fume. Zandstra releases his cigarette onto the driveway, twists his leather-soled toe across the burning ember, crunching the loose gravel.

Pash cycles up towards the porte-cochère. He dismounts, leans the bicycle against the side of the house and bends down to collect his gardening tools when he sees Zandstra.

'Afternoon, Sir,' says Pash.

'Ah, you. What part of your work do you like best, boy?' asks Zandstra.

'The gardens, Sir,' answers Pash.

'The gardens, well, I have a beautiful garden. You must come sometime and see it for yourself,' says Zandstra. 'What is your name, young man?'

'Sir,' says Pash.

'Your name!' says Zandstra.

'Pash, Sir,' says Pash.

'Come, after you are finished here, Pash, and I will show you my garden,' says Zandstra.

A few hours pass and I keep busy, sweeping quietly behind the front doors until I see Zandstra make his way out of the house and down the lane towards the front gates. Pash follows him and my heart sinks. I know this is not good.

'Boy! Ah good, you are still here. You waited. Let us go. To the gardens!' slurs Zandstra.

'Yes, Sir,' says Pash.

Zandstra puts his arm around Pash and they walk out and down towards Malcolm Road.

After seeing Pash leave with Zandstra, my imagination goes to a dark place and I can't concentrate on my chores. That afternoon, I have a stack of table linens to iron and fold. The hot iron wobbles on the ironing board and as it falls over, I reach for it, burning the soft part of my arm, before it hits the floor. The wound is deep, and for weeks, as layer after layer of skin bubbles and grows over, I feel my heart hardening. I try to fight this feeling by reaching for my imagination to help me stop the closing happiness, but I can feel it, my loss of hope.

My injury means I am relieved of the heavy lifting of laundry and I am tasked with moving inside the house more often, where I can manage light dusting. Ma'am is lying on the chaise lounge in the living room one afternoon. I don't hear her or even notice she is there, until, she starts to laugh. Quietly at first, then in a maniacal way.

'You really are hopeless,' she says.

'Ma'am,' I say.

'How'd you injure yourself? Caught the blooming iron? What an idiot, what an absolute idiot,' says Ma'am. 'I mean, you do understand the iron is hot, you do, don't you? I . . . I just can't imagine such idiocy.'

I feel my face start to burn and keep away from her sharp words.

'Useless girl. Turn the radio on!' Ma'am demands. 'I want to hear the news. And get me a gin and tonic!'

'Ma'am, I . . .' I begin.

'All right then, call Vee to make me one,' demands Ma'am.

'Yes, Ma'am,' I say.

I find Vee who arrives and makes Ma'am her drink. In between the clink of ice against glass, I can make out more news on the radio about Maria and the woman who has been caring for her all these years, Che Aminah. The voice on the radio mentions words like 'the parents' and 'the courts' and how now 'other countries are getting involved'.

'Turn it up, would you?' asks Ma'am.

Vee moves quickly towards the radio and in her rush, she may have pushed the knob too hard or turned it too quickly or the table leg may have been too weak, the reasoning doesn't matter, but the radio falls off the table and crashes to the floor, leaving a dent in the wooden casing.

'What the hell?!' screams Ma'am, goes over to Vee, and slaps her.

I stand back in shock. Ma'am has slapped Vee, the kindest of us all, a person who would never harm another.

'Get out of my face!' screams Ma'am.

Vee and I turn to pick up the radio off the floor.

'I. Said. Out!' she screams.

Her voice rises to a sound I haven't heard before. It is a level of sound that is jagged and orange and green and smells of fear. I wonder what is making her so angry, then I remember Zandstra and Pash walking together and realize that Ma'am has been replaced.

'Ma'am, I didn't, she didn't . . .' I say.

'You, don't talk to me. You're just good for one thing, watching out for me. Do you understand?' says Ma'am.

I turn from her and gather my cleaning supplies and the feather duster and follow Vee out of the room when Ma'am calls to my back.

'You like him, don't you. Pash, he's handsome, isn't he? I've seen you out in the garden speaking with him. Well, he's spoken for, you can forget Pash,' she says laughing. 'Spoken for!'

I rush away from her and down to the servants' quarters. I sit with Vee on her bed for a few minutes, wondering what to do. I hold on to Vee's hands as she cries into her lap.

'Was accident,' says Vee.

'I know, it's fine, don't worry,' I tell her.

'My face, it hurts. Will I be let go?' asks Vee.

'No, nothing like that, everything will be fine,' I say.

We hear sweeping outside the servants' quarters.

'Pash?' I call out through Vee's window.

I've never called his name out loud, only in my private thoughts.

'Mei Mei?' Pash answers.

'Can you come? Vee, she needs help!' I say.

Before he comes around to Vee's bedroom door, Vee speaks to me in a still, quiet voice.

'You can't know, you can't know why people act, and act cruel, remember that, don't blame others, we are all slightly angry most of the time,' says Vee.

'What happened?' asks Pash as he appears at the door. He kneels in front of the cot. He puts his hands on top of mine holding hers.

'Ma'am got angry and hit Vee,' I say, still amazed at Vee and what she has told me and that Pash is holding our hands.

'Un... unacceptable,' says Pash. 'No, not good, I am going to...'

'Leave it now, I am all right, leave it, nothing can be done,' says Vee.

'Mei Mei,' says Pash, 'thank you for helping my aunt.'

I smile and blush and cherish his voice calling my name and hope I don't become a person who is angry most of the time.

The next morning, I am in the kitchen with Vee. I hear the sound of flapping and I see a hornbill crowding the backdoor. It looks dazed and is dragging its wing, its huge bill is cracked.

'A hornbill!' says Vee. 'Oh, it's injured. Mei Mei, bring a clean towel, but move slowly.'

I am amazed by the size of this bird. Of course, I have seen them high up in the trees, watched as they flit from canopy to canopy, their wings motoring them forward in straight lines from rooftop to treetop, heard their calls to one another, but I've never seen one close up like this. It is beautiful.

'Mei Mei, come now . . . help,' says Vee.

I gather a towel and sheets. Vee carefully scoops the injured bird up onto her lap. It flaps and twists its body trying to get away.

'Help me hold it still,' she says.

I am both intrigued and terrified by the size of this wild bird. Its bones feel brittle yet strong, its breathing is rapid.

'A messenger,' says Vee. 'A messenger from Heaven to earth, a symbol. Here, you hold it, I'll find a box we can place it in, careful now, don't hold it too tight,' says Vee.

I sit alone in the kitchen house with this enormous bird on my lap. It is almost as big as me. It heaves with fear and I wonder who is more afraid, me or this majestic bird. What does Vee mean, a messenger? I imagine this bird has come to tell us to fly, to imagine a future beyond this house, and just then a slight breeze brings in the familiar smell of sickly sweetness and heat mixed with sweat. Zandstra. I look out and see him standing at the edge of the garden. He is holding the swimming pool pole, thrashing the space in the trees where the hornbills make their nests.

Ling Li comes across the walkway carrying silverware in from the main house.

'What's this? So huge?' says Ling Li.

'Ssshhh, Ling Li, you'll frighten it, it's already terrified,' I say.

'What you doing? Good as dead, why bring a dead bird inside?' says Ling Li.

'I can mend, we can, I'll call Pash,' I say.

'Don't bother with it, help me with the silver polishing,' says Ling Li.

'I will later,' I say.

Ling Li clicks her tongue.

'Later, later,' says Ling Li under her breath.

Pash and Honour have been cycling in the gardens and come to the kitchen house.

'Zandstra, he's . . . Wah! A hornbill! It's enormous. You know it's a sign of good luck,' says Pash.

'Or bad luck, it's injured,' I say.

Vee returns with a large box. Pash and I carry the bird and place it, with Vee's help, into the box onto the table in the kitchen house.

'He's breathing so fast, look, look his eyes, he looks afraid,' says Pash.

'He? How do you know he's a he?' I ask.

The bird retreats into the far corners of the box, fluttering its good wing against the sides. We hear a whistling sound from its cracked beak and its claws scratch the box.

'Water, it'll need water,' says Honour.

'How do they even drink?' I ask.

'Let me squeeze a cloth of water against its beak, maybe it can use its tongue?' says Pash.

'It's so huge,' says Honour.

'It's so beautiful,' I say. 'Zandstra . . . he was . . .'

'This is probably the male, the male feeds the female who is inside the nest, packed in with mud, with the eggs. If the male doesn't get back to her, she will starve and won't be able to feed her chicks when they hatch.'

'And Zandstra just destroyed the nest,' says Honour.

'A widower bird now,' says Pash.

'It'll heal itself or die,' I say.

Sir comes around to our gathering in the kitchen house.

'What have we got here?' asks Sir.

'Hornbill, Sir,' says Pash.

'That's extraordinary. How did you . . .?' asks Sir.

'I think it's trying to tell us something,' I say.

'What, Mei Mei?' asks Sir.

'Beware of Zandstra, Sir, that's what it is telling,' I say.

'What she means is . . .' begins Honour.

'It's all right, I know exactly what you mean, Mei Mei,' says Sir. 'I need to deal with this.'

Sir is off, striding across the garden where Zandstra stands with the pool pole. Sir grabs it from him and shoves Zandstra across his chest with the pole.

'Off. Get off! You're a beast. Now! Go and dry out, Zandstra,' shouts Sir.

None of us have ever seen Sir like this, showing his power and strength. He has always been such a gentleman. The three of us share a secret grin. Sir has had enough and Zandstra is no longer welcome at the house. We all feel relief, but what fools we are. It only makes Zandstra more unkind and more determined to dominate us all, and, within a day, our magical bird is dead.

Chapter Fourteen

MEI MEI

1950

Singapore

My imagination is being fuelled by images of hornbills as messengers from Heaven to earth. It keeps me entertained as I work—cleaning the house, doing endless laundry. I am unprepared for Honour to be interested in anything mystical, but she surprises me with an interest in our shrine, where Ling Li and I burn joss sticks and paper effigies to the ancestors.

'Do you believe in ghosts?' asks Honour.

'Ghosts?' I ask.

'Yes, ghosts,' says Honour.

'Well, we keep them happy, this is what we do,' I say.

'So, have you seen any? Here at the house, have you seen any?' asks Honour.

'Why you want to see a ghost?' I ask.

'Don't you?' asks Honour.

'We live with them,' I say.

'What do you mean?' asks Honour.

'The hungry ghosts, they want something from the living and we must listen,' I say.

Honour laughs. 'There's no such thing,' she says.

'Yes, there is,' I say.

'So, what do they look like?' Honour asks.

'It's not so much what they look like, more that they are always here with us. I send them what they need in the next life, you know, clothes, a car,' I tell her.

'What for? That's ridiculous. They're dead, why would they need anything?' says Honour.

'That's our job as the living to give to our ancestors what they need,' I tell her.

'Aunt Faith tells me you are all superstitious and not to believe all this about your shrines and gods. My God would never let ghosts appear, that's all nonsense,' says Honour.

I want to believe in Honour's God, who does not demand any offerings. It is much cleaner. For me, it is a full-time job, keeping up with all the festival days and keeping certain family members in the underworld happy and none of the family members are even mine.

'Just different, we are just different. Hungry ghosts exist,' I say. 'What about you, have you seen a ghost back in England?'

'Well, some of the girls in boarding school saw them, yes,' Honour says.

'Have you seen them?' I ask.

'No,' says Honour. 'But I felt them, they were there, I swear.'

'Tell me then, what did the other girls see?' I ask.

'The school, where I studied . . . it was once a castle—for wealthy relatives of Aunt Faith's. There is a space under the chapel for the crypt,' says Honour.

'Chapel? Crypt?' I ask.

'Where they bury the dead,' says Honour.

'And?' I ask.

'The ghosts, I felt them come at me and they terrorized me just like the ghosts here will!' says Honour.

Honour leaps up, grabs me by my shoulders, and starts to howl the way she thinks a ghost might sound. I let out a scream and we both start shrieking with laughter and fear. I am so surprised by her action that I laugh and laugh until I have trouble breathing again.

'I want to see ghosts here!' Honour demands. 'Show me, how can I see them?'

'We can visit the feng shui master, he can show you how,' I say.

The shophouses on the main part of Emerald Hill are decorated with colourful tiles featuring pastel ornamentations of birds and flowers favoured by the Peranakan style. In contrast, the laneways behind these colourful houses hold makeshift shelters where large families scarred by the ruins of the war live without toilets. It is chaotic. Random building supplies lean against walls to form rooms where multiple generations live in this rubble: a massive contrast to the estate where we live, where Aunt Faith's family, the Ducharmes', fortune has been made by the worldwide demand for rubber, tin, and shipping, all industries in which my employer, Angus Hamilton, is a senior player.

Looking for the feng shui master's apartment, we find a corner house on Saunders Road. It is lemon yellow with rose pink and pale blue tiles featuring hand-painted images of birds. Children gather around us, touching Honour's dress until a woman guides us to a large wooden door. We are ushered to the second floor and invited to sit and wait. Large windows face the street and are covered with heavy wooden shutters closed tight against the beating sun. We turn in the direction of a door opening in anticipation of meeting the master. I hear a familiar voice and gasp.

'Aunt Faith?' I mouth the words to Honour and pull her towards me. We hide behind an ornately carved privacy screen.

'Thank you, Grand Master Tong, I am grateful and hope for a positive outcome for all,' says Aunt Faith in Hokkien.

Honour and I are face to face behind the screen with our mouths open.

'It's Aunt Faith,' Honour mouths to me in silence.

I nod, then shrug. We wait a few minutes until we sense Aunt Faith has left the shophouse. We hear a young male attendant call us. We step out from behind the screen and are guided into a room where Master Tong sits on a low stool.

'Mei Mei! And you've brought a friend!' he says.

'My mistress, Miss Honour, Sir,' I say.

'How can I help you?' he asks.

'Was that my aunt, Faith Ducharmes?' asks Honour.

'Ms Ducharmes is a regular customer, ah, yes. We do regular business together,' he says.

'I-I didn't realize,' says Honour.

'What happens here, ah, who comes for my expertise is private, you understand this, yes? Young ladies?' he says. 'Now, how can I help?'

'I want to see a ghost,' says Honour.

'Aija,' Master Tong breathes in through his teeth and clucks his tongue, smacks his open palm on his knees.

'Why the young push the underworld, lah?' he asks.

'What do you mean, Sir?' asks Honour.

'Asking to see a ghost is not something you demand,' he says.

'But I pay,' says Honour.

Master Tong slouches and sighs. Closing his eyes, he continues. 'Do you feel cold or sharp headache when you go inside house?' he asks.

'Why are you asking?' says Honour.

'Only harmful ghosts make problem,' he says.

'Well, no, no, then I'm fine, no problems,' says Honour.

'You must be careful, Miss. Don't press the underworld. You can try to change your qi, your energy,' he says.

'My energy?' asks Honour.

'Tell me your birth date. What day you born, what year?' he asks.

Master Tong gathers numbers, locations, lists of months and days, details I never knew would be of much interest to anyone. He consults charts and uses special instruments to measure numbers on what looks like an astrological atlas.

'Your qi, hard to read. I can try the face,' he begins. 'Face have mountains and rivers, shows good fortune.'

'My face has mountains and rivers? That's ridiculous!' says Honour.

'Hush,' he says.

He looks at Honour's face, starting with her forehead, her eyes, nose, chin, and cheekbones.

'You have an unlucky face. Your eyes, you not sleeping? You need to make your eyes shine, see, like Mei Mei here,' he says to Honour.

'What?' asks Honour.

'She has mark on her face, yes, everyone can see that, but it's her eyes, her eyes are powerful,' he says.

'You, yours, your eyes are not clear, you not sure where you belong. You are . . . rootless,' he says.

Master Tong goes on to tell us to go home and that he doesn't want our money, but Honour waves his hands away and gives it to him anyway. The incense and darkness in the room make me feel claustrophobic and I need some air. I lurch forward and out of the room, and follow the steps leading up to the roof. Honour follows and we stand together overlooking Emerald Hill and Orchard Road, watching the rows of shophouses, people walking in and amongst them. I see a myriad of colours, strong and vibrant.

'He's old, no need to pay attention,' I say to Honour.

'But he's right, I'm lost and I don't really belong here anyway,' she says.

'Don't mind him,' I say.

'You heard the old man, I don't have enough qi, I won't have any fortune. I just don't belong here. I have nothing, rootless,' she says.

'Maybe, but you have wings,' I tell her.

As we stand on the roof, the sun starts to set. Flocks of black-naped orioles gather in the tops of trees, their bodies shining bronze, their calls announcing the beginning of dusk to one another. Master Tong joins us on the roof and we watch the sun set through the filigree green boughs of the trees bowing under the weight of the birds. This friendship with my mistress is such a strange thing. I feel an ache at the back of my heart, an ache I know will only grow with time.

Back at the house, we walk through the courtyard and see Pash standing with his back to us. Sweat collects along his spine, his back muscles twitch as he tightens his lungi firmly across his hips. He turns to us and smiles. I admire his body, his clean face, his strong jaw, he truly is a beauty. I touch my face where I know the stain is and watch as Honour moves towards him, exaggerating the curve of her waist, her hand on her hip, she angles her head and looks up at him.

'How are the gardens? My aunt's roses?' she asks.

'Fine, they have thorns but lovely buds,' says Pash.

'Can I see?' she asks. She has sweetened her voice.

'Come.' He offers Honour to join him to see the pots he is keeping for Ma'am.

'I hear Ling Li calling you,' Honour says to me and I know I am not welcome.

In the sanctity of my room, I locate new parts of myself. I sit on my cot and watch my reflection over my shoulder as I take off my work dress one shoulder at a time, tugging at the damp cloth. I imagine Pash taking off my clothes and as I turn directly to the mirror, I rip down my own dress, pressing my hands against my breasts, moving my fingers up over my face, closing my eyes.

'Yes, yes, take me now, now, yes . . .' I whisper.

'Mei Mei!' Honour is standing by the door to my room. 'What . . . are you doing?' she asks.

'Getting changed,' my face reddens and I put my dress back on.

I move out to the hallway and keel in front of the makeshift shrine I have built with Ling Li and start to burn Hell banknotes.

'What were you just doing?' she asks.

'Praying,' I say.

'Doesn't look like praying to me,' says Honour.

'What does it matter?' I say.

'What for then? What are you praying for? For Pash? For Pash to come and give you some love and attention?' Honour makes a kissing sound.

'For peace and safe passage,' I say.

'That's rubbish,' says Honour.

'Not to me,' I say and move back into my room shrugging her presence away.

Honour follows me into my room. 'All of this, rubbish!' she says, gesturing towards the incense. She looks around, twists her face, and reaches for my doll on my bed. I grab my doll from her and, in one movement, lift up its dress and turn it over. With the knife Ling Li uses to open the packages of joss sticks, I make a clean slice down the back of my doll's plastic cavity and banknotes spill out.

'What are you doing?' screams Honour.

'Go away!' I say.

'What's all this?' she asks.

'Not your business,' I tell her.

'Tell me!' she demands.

'Money!' I scream.

'Who gave you all that money? Who's it for?' she asks. 'How much is that?'

'Go away! Spirits don't like,' I say.

'Spirits don't like,' she copies my voice and intonation. 'Spirits don't like what, the paper money?'

'It's real to the spirits,' I say.

'So then, why don't you burn the real money? I dare you, I dare you, burn the real money!' she says.

'Cannot!' I say.

'Why not? Isn't real money more real? Then your ancestors can bloody well really use it?' she starts yelling.

'Not your place,' I say.

'It bloody well is,' says Honour.

She grabs at the bills Ma'am has paid me and throws them into the little shrine. A few bills are set alight and the flames start to grow.

'No!' I yell and grab the burning money. 'That's real money!' I scream.

'What's real, what's not real, Mei Mei?' screams Honour.

'Your aunt give me that money, she give money to watch when she goes with Zandstra,' I say.

'What?' Honour stops. 'She's been with him before?' asks Honour.

'Yes, and others,' I say.

Honour starts to gasp for air. She lurches forward to take the bills from me. I come at Honour with a fistful of incense sticks and throw them towards her.

'No!' I scream and knock her over.

Honour starts to scream.

'Honour?' A voice comes out from the darkness. 'Girls! Girls!'

It is Ma'am's voice.

'Ma'am!' I say.

'What is going on here?' demands Ma'am.

Ma'am turns to me and shakes her head. I feel deep shame.

'Honour, come with me, stay well away from that girl,' says Ma'am.

I use my blanket to stop the burning fire. Honour makes me so angry, but she is the closest thing I have ever had to a friend. I sit on the edge of my cot and cry. I am surrounded by ash and smoke and I am back to where I was before she came, friendless.

The next morning is Monday and I wonder how I can avoid Honour. It is already so humid and I dread the work piling up. I can't get any drying done on the line today. Lying still on my cot, I hear the familiar sweeping sound outside my window. I know it is not Pash. It is Siti, the old Malay woman who sometimes comes to help. Her hair is pulled back into a neat bun, her left hand is balanced like a bird on the small of her back while, with her right arm, she sweeps the fallen leaves in a balletic motion, the rhythm easing into a reassuring, restful brushing sound. She gathers the leaves in a woven basket and burns them at the back of the garden. The rooster crows. He pecks away in the undergrowth with the other jungle fowl. Then the koel sounds the start of another day.

Chapter Fifteen

MEI MEI

September 1950

Cameron Highlands, Malaya

It is to be the full eclipse of the sun, and the Cameron Highlands in Malaya, a day's drive from Singapore, is the best spot in the region to view the shifting shape of the sun. Suleiman tells me he will take Sir and Honour. They are to be hosted by the Jesus people at a Christian Mission's Young Men's Mechanical School, where Pash will be staying for a week. I hear Honour and Angus making plans.

'We're guests of Miss Isabelle Griffith-Jones, Aunt Faith's friend,' says Sir. 'Why not bring Mei Mei?'

'Mei Mei?' asks Honour.

'Ja, Mei Mei. She could use a break, a trip,' says Sir.

'Bad idea,' says Honour.

'Bad idea or not, she's coming, she needs a break just like everyone else,' says Sir.

Ma'am is furious that I am going on the trip with Honour and Sir.

'Why didn't you check with me first, Angus?' asks Ma'am. 'What'll I do?'

'You've got Ling Li and Vee to help, just rest, you'll need your energy,' says Sir.

'Well . . .' says Ma'am.

'And Mei Mei, needs a break,' says Sir.

'Ha, what?' asks Ma'am.

'Yes, Tessa, children. She's a child,' says Sir.

'She is well taken care of, I assure you,' says Ma'am.

'Right, running up and down with your washing,' says Sir.

'Where's this all coming from Angus?' says Ma'am.

'I've seen the two of them together,' says Sir.

'Two of whom?' says Ma'am.

'Honour, with Mei Mei, they seem like friends,' says Sir.

'Ha! Not likely, they—' begins Ma'am.

'Yes, friends,' interrupts Sir.

'And you want to encourage this, do you, this . . . whatever it is, friendship?' asks Ma'am.

'Tessa, they're children. Is friendship so wrong?' asks Sir.

'The way things are going with the Hertogh trial, yes, it *is* wrong. We should keep them separate,' says Ma'am.

'How is them being separated going to affect the court ruling? It's a fait accompli,' says Sir.

'You think the courts will rule in favour of the Hertoghs?' asks Ma'am.

'I know so,' says Sir.

'And you think heading off to the Cameron Highlands now, during the verdict, is a good idea? There will be mobs, who knows communist insurgents, you'll be a sitting duck,' says Ma'am.

'We'll be fine. Suleiman knows the roads,' says Sir.

'All right, take the girls,' says Ma'am. 'Let Honour have Mei Mei. I'll have Vee and Ling Li to look after me, I won't be doing much!'

On the drive up to the Highlands, Suleiman and I listen as Sir and Honour take turns breaking into song in their best radio voices. 'And did those feet in ancient time / Walk upon Englands mountains green . . .' Suleiman looks back at them, wraps his fingers around the steering wheel, fidgeting his thumbs back and forth, then casting a side-glance at me he shakes his head bemused as Sir and Honour keep their voices low crossing into Johor then raise them high again as the roads open wide.

I notice the roads are uneven and the buildings are either being torn down or built up after the Japanese occupation. We drive for what seems like days through palm plantations and then start to move up the winding roads into the mountains, where tea plantations and rice paddies rise from the corners of the view like ripples of green ocean tide. 'Till we have built Jerusalem / In Englands green and pleasant Land.' I copy their voices, humming to myself. The humidity lifts. Their voices subside.

As we approach the village near the mission school, the sun starts to set and groups of women congregate along the sides of the road, meeting one another while heading into villages tucked into the mountains. It is dark when we arrive. The next day is to be the eclipse. Honour has managed to ignore me the whole way.

In the morning, Sir takes Honour through the small *kampong*. I follow along behind them. We hear quiet drumming coming from inside the villagers' small homes, we see no people. Newspapers line the windows and not even a stray dog roams the red-soil roads. Sir tells us that people from this village were convinced that the solar eclipse is a bad omen: that the sun being blocked by its own reflection is unnatural, that the devil is present, and that children are cursed if allowed to go outside.

'*Will* they be cursed, Uncle?' Honour asks.

'You don't believe this, do you, Honour?' asks Sir.

'Will *I* be cursed?' she asks.

'No one knows for certain what change the eclipse will bring, but it will alter us, Honour. You can feel it, Mei Mei . . . can't you?' asks Sir.

Back at the guesthouse of the Mission School, the staff fill up large buckets of water for people to view the reflection of the eclipse. We gather around the metal tubs, half expecting nothing to happen. It seems absurd that in the heat of the day, the sun will disappear.

As it gets darker, I look for Pash everywhere. Is he really here? What does he think of this place, this magical hill? I can't help but imagine us together, him being forever grateful to me for helping Vee.

Gradually, as if a dark monsoon cloud has gathered overhead, the midday light slips away as a crescent-shaped disk begins to cover the bright sun. Sir and Honour watch the reflection in the water until even the fine lines of the eclipse are invisible. I look deep into the dark water, pressing my eyelids closed then open them again to see what I had known to be there, but the harder I look, the more darkness I feel. There are no stars.

It is then that I feel a finger caress a line down the front of my hand. The finger makes its way to the soft inside of my palm, then enters, searching, prodding for a response. I freeze and let my hand stretch open to this set of fingers that interlace with mine, pulse, and then let go. I stand perfectly still in the dark. It is my first seduction.

Despite how gradually darkness fell, the sun starts to regain its foothold, and soon after, I am back in full blazing sunlight. Standing next to me is Pash. He is smiling. I stare at his face and find his pupils. They are surrounded with a warm, green-brown hue and the whites of his eyes are so clear. I pull back my gaze slightly to see his dark lashes and the ridge of his nose. His eyes are set so deep that they draw me in. I imagine his long, fine nose nudging me, his lips searching for mine, his nose breathing across my cheek.

On the long drive back to Singapore, I relieve myself in the sugar cane fields and find that I have become a woman. I still have many hours of sitting in the car with Sir and Honour and Suleiman. I keep my knees pressed tight the whole way home reliving the sensory memory of Pash's fingers in mine.

Back in my shared room with Ling Li, I can't sleep. I walk out to the walkway and smell cigarette smoke. Honour is trying to light a cigarette. The other staff have the night off and we are alone with no sounds from the sleeping quarters and no lights from the kitchen. Honour has a small kerosene light near her feet.

'Can't sleep,' says Honour.

'Me neither,' I say.

'I found my aunt's cigarettes, want to try?' asks Honour.

'How do I?' I ask

'Here,' says Honour and flicks open a lighter.

I don't know how to inhale the proper way, and I cough and splutter. Honour starts to laugh. I laugh back. We both laugh so hard, we fall over, holding our cigarettes high above our heads. I feel warmth and connection and blotches of gold flecks wash above me in my mind.

'I'm in love,' says Honour, 'with Pash.'

I stop laughing and sit up straight. The colours go dark and I feel bile rise from my gut. *No, no, no. He's mine*, I say to myself.

Chapter Sixteen

ISABELLE GOH

1999

London

Detective, I was the type of child you'd never notice. I had perfected being invisible yet always there when needed. No one would ever imagine that I had an actual opinion or thought of my own and that I was in love with Pash. Yet with each load of laundry, I was growing into a woman on the landing.

Moving my hands over my hips and across my chest, I marvel at how my breasts are forming. I map new contours on my body, mesmerized by the direction of the water when I bathe. I watch as it flows along new trails on my figure with its hidden crevasses and new depths. I twist and angle my spine, transforming the water into gentle tides. I wonder what Pash would feel like if I were to touch his shoulders. I imagine his arms wrapped around me. I practise kissing my knee caps, imagining him close.

I adjust to this reality of Honour and Pash and me living and working at the house. But I am starting to feel uneasy, a disease.

So many secrets. Ma'am from Sir. Zandstra from Sir. Me from Ling Li. But what is mapped on top of my unease is a sense of envy. I am burning with envy. I want everything Honour has. Why does she get to have Pash on top of all the things she has? I want her to leave me a piece of her world.

One Sunday evening before the sun sets, I make my way to the fort Honour and I have built above the stone courtyard and stand overlooking the roof of the estate, the intersections of the sleeping rooms, the covered walkway, and the servants' quarters. From there, I can see the mosque, the enormous rain trees and vast tracts of jungle tops, green shades, a patchwork of leaves of every known shape and size. A true jungle paradise. I feel like I can see forever. I watch dusk begin to close the sky with orange and purple turning to blue with a tinge of pink then hear the crickets subside and the koel begin her call.

I move a little further from our special perch over the stone garden near Sir's study to watch Pash. He moves like a panther, each step deliberate and paced. He holds himself so erect, his neck straight. His height gives him an elegance and he is aware of how his body moves. People react to him with respect. I stand there, admiring Pash and his calm movements.

I look up and over the rooftops and I can see the curve of the lane down Chancery Lane to Gentle Drive. The lights inside the black-and-white houses are filtered through the deep green of the jungle. I see the officers' quarters, some seven bedrooms long, then the road rises and curves, the houses become larger, grander, with vast tracts of land, of open grass surfacing around and amongst the jungle.

I can feel people moving about. Sir walks out of his study, waiting for his cocktail in the mission chairs on the garden veranda. I can, from my space in the sky, hear his choice of music, soft, gentle classical music. I can feel Ma'am's lost attention. She is drawing a coral-coloured pencil over her lips, extra thick and wide, elongating her smile, licking her lips to appear more appealing as she sucks the ice and mint and lemon and gin.

I feel the heartache of Vee as she recovers from the miscarriage. A wedge of cotton towels between her knees I will wash later. I sense the tension of Cook. How he secretly supports his brothers, hiding out in the mountains of Malaysia, how they tell him he is a slave to the colonialists. He sets a timer for his cooking and during the countdown of the seconds, wonders what his brothers eat as they play the role of taking down the rubber barons. I see each person in the estate making their private supplications to their own Gods: Ganesha, Allah, Jesus Christ, and the ancestors.

I see Honour in my imagination. She is taller, firm waisted, her hair shorter, to her chin, her eyelids hooded and her gaze pointed. I see her walk up behind Pash and lock her arms around his back. I see him close his eyes and tilt his head back with pleasure as she presses herself close to him. He turns to her, searching for her face.

Up in the fort where I am observing the evening and imagining the future, I hear someone coming and feel my body being pushed, once, twice, and as I turn to look, Honour shoves me over the edge of our perch and I fall. I remember reaching forward in the air, grasping, then crushing pain and loss of breath. Black out.

Part II

DISGUISE

Chapter Seventeen

MEI MEI

November 1950

Singapore

The injury to my face is severe enough to need surgery to repair my split lip, and the concussion means I have a lengthy hospital stay. My eyes are black and blue and no one apart from Ling Li comes to visit me.

'How did you fall?' asks the nurse with the soft hands.

She asks without wanting an answer. She moves about my hospital bed, rearranging a clean towel near my face to help catch any spittle. I want to speak, but my mouth aches.

'Mind you, don't make any trouble,' says the nurse who smells like sandalwood. She speaks slowly to me. 'Be careful.'

'You should heal fast,' says the nurse with the soft hands.

The nurses speak to each other as if I am not there. They talk about the lost and found girl, Maria, the trouble that is brewing. I sense their fear. It has a colour: ashtray grey.

The first few nights when my pain is deepest, the nurse who smells like sandalwood combs out my hair. It is matted from the blood and the humidity.

'She pushed me,' I say slowly, moving the words around in my mouth.

'But why, why did you let her push you, lah?' the nurse with the soft hands whispers.

I never do answer. The confusion in my heart is too deep, my sadness too wide.

Later that night, I start to have my first violent thoughts. I pray to the Jesus lady's God to take them away, but I start to think of hurtful things to get back at Honour. I don't understand that what is happening to me is greed and envy and covetousness. I channel this hatred, this anger at being taken advantage of, being tossed aside, and keep it as fuel for when I am older.

On the other side of my curtain, I overhear women talking about Maria. *Maria, Maria.* I wonder what she must be feeling, pushed around by different people. The courts, her own parents. I feel a deep connection to this girl I have never known.

'That poor young girl, taken like that,' says a woman with a slight lisp.

'The English courts are right to try this case,' says another voice, strong and opinionated sounding.

'She belongs with her true family,' says the other. 'But, what if, what if her own mother can't recognize her?'

'My biggest nightmare—imagine, not recognizing your own child,' says the forceful one. 'I don't know what I'd do.'

I turn towards the curtain and, with a weak but clear voice, share my thoughts.

'What if . . .' I begin. 'What if Maria doesn't want her mother? What if she wants to stay with her husband and Che Aminah?'

The women part the curtain and when they see me, they look at each other, and their faces redden. I sense a feeling I haven't felt before. These women would kill to defend their own children. I read this emotion as a colour. It is a mix of black and red all jumbled together into angry, coloured letters that leap out from the tops of their heads. These letters of anger then fill my head and I become infected.

The night when the pain is at its worst, Ling Li comes and stands beside my bed. 'You will be better soon, much work to do,' says Ling Li.

The work, the endless work. I don't know if I can go back to such a life, a life where I am just a servant girl.

'Ma'am going to have a baby, she will need an extra pair of hands,' says Ling Li.

'A baby?' I ask.

'Yes, yes, you get better, then you can help with the baby,' says Ling Li.

I don't fully understand the ins and outs of baby making. All I know is what I see Ma'am do with the men and what happens to the street dogs who get onto the property some days. The locking of their bodies, and the swelling of the belly of the female dog and the puppies that follow. How can I tell Ling Li about what really happened, about the push, the men, the real money, and the evil of Honour and Ma'am and Zandstra, not me? No one will listen, no one will care. The one thing that gives me a tinge of happiness is that Ling Li says Pash asks about me. Pash, my Pash. The colour I see when she speaks about Pash is cream, always silky cream.

Five weeks after the fall, my teeth are still blackened. The skin under my nose above my lip is thin from multiple surgeries. Ling Li is wearing a new blouse and a stranger appears in the kitchen house. Ling Li blushes when she introduces him to me. He has a bald head and high cheekbones. This man seems fearless to me. He speaks his mind.

'I'm Mr Today, want to make my day?' he says.

I recoil at his forwardness and am surprised to see Ling Li giggle.

'What an idiot,' she remarks waving him away with a limp wrist.

'It's a catchy name,' he insists. 'What do you think?'

'You stay well away from him, Mei Mei. He will make himself millions, but he is dangerous,' says Ling Li.

I am attracted to the idea of millions—if it is real money, and money I can keep.

'She's the one I told you about,' says Ling Li to Mr Today.

'Oh, the guppy, you found under the docks,' he says. 'Come here, let me take a look at you.'

I move slowly and stand beside Ling Li.

'Pity about her face, otherwise a nice-looking girl,' he says.

'Never mind, ah, she's a hard worker,' says Ling Li.

I am immediately wary of this flattery. What is Ling Li doing, talking about me with a complete stranger?

'Her money saved from her hard work. She can help you grow your business,' says Ling Li.

What does she mean my money could help his business? I am really steaming now.

'You know your cousin, Su Yin, has done well. She has her own house now, in Ipoh, and her son is entering secondary school. She helps me,' Mr Today tells Ling Li.

'Yes, she has done well for herself,' says Ling Li. 'Mei Mei, hear him out. Mr Today has a business proposal.'

A business proposal. I don't understand.

'I'm looking for help. Demand is high for good servants in the houses of the wealthy Chinese and Europeans,' says Mr Today.

'And?' I ask.

'I am starting a delivery service, of girls. I need someone like you who can talk to these girls and prepare them to work in Singapore,' says Mr Today.

Absolutely not. There is no way. I need to follow the tracks Pash and Honour are making and erase them.

'No, my money, is my money,' I say.

I will never help this man. I run into the main house with a bucket to clean and towels to fold, but while running away, I am intrigued.

After Mr Today's visit to the kitchen house, everything shifts. The story of Maria is still in people's minds and there seems to be tension inside and outside the gates. No one seems to be able to do anything right. Ma'am is always angry, it seems she mirrors what is on the radio news. People are spitting threats and calculating errors, tabulating harms, no one can do anything right, everyone shouts hatred at people's feet.

We are all jealous. What I want, I can never have, never become. I desire everything that Honour has. Pash is mine, I want him and don't want anyone else touching him, least of all Honour. I see Honour flaunting her body in front of me. I channel this envy into my heart and it starts to grow into a slow burning flame.

The first time I see Honour again, after the push, she is gliding underwater like a colourful fish, her dark hair waving behind her. I have come down to deliver towels and drinks by the pool. The sun is glaring and I stand behind in the shade watching her. Pash is working near the pool. He is bare chested. He catches Honour looking at him, then she looks away bashfully. Pash can't help himself. He removes his lungi and slips into the deep end in the shade and waits for her to draw closer.

Pash reaches for her hand, holds it underwater then swims away. He is lithe in the water, coming up for air with his body polished. Water pools in the hollows of his shoulders, where they expand away from his chest. I watch as Honour swims up to him and laps up the water that collects there, she teases him with her eyes. Pash dives down and when he comes up for air, he is face to face with Honour. Pash smiles and Honour moves his hand down between her legs, pressing it against her private centre. Pash's hands make love to her, each finger strokes and gently pulses, while the water laps over the edge.

I can't look away from my place in the shade and am startled when she climbs out of the pool in one lunge. I hold up my hand as a greeting and she looks right through me. She gathers her hair across her shoulder, twists the water out, and wraps a towel around her. Together, Pash and Honour walk back up to the house, leaving me standing there like a fool.

The day I see sand on the floor of the car, I know Honour has been with Pash, my darling Pash. Suleiman is teaching Pash to drive and takes him to Pasir Ris. I soon realize that Honour joins and Suleiman leaves them at the beach to suck and twist and breathe. I know by the stains on Honour's clothes that they are intimate.

'I'm in,' I tell Ling Li.

'What you mean?' she asks.

'I mean, I'm in, I'll put my money, all of it, into Mr Today's business, I want to get rich.' *And have Pash for myself*, I say inside my head. 'What do I have to do?'

'It will be dangerous,' says Ling Li pressing her hand against her tattoo. 'Are you sure, Mei Mei, once you take a step in this direction, you can never come back.'

'I need more, I can't stay here forever,' I tell her.

'It's not a bad life,' she tells me. 'This one. Here at the house, it is safe.'

'It's not safe,' I blurt. 'Zandstra, he . . .'

Ling Li laughs.

'Zandstra? You, you afraid of Zandstra? Let me tell you, he is cruel and can't keep his pants on, but there are far worse people out there, far worse,' says Ling Li.

'Well . . .' I start to say.

'There's not much I can say that you will listen to,' says Ling Li.

'I've decided, I'll agree and work with Mr Today,' I tell her.

'Wait until after the baby comes, then we'll see what you decide,' says Ling Li.

Mr Today makes another appearance in the kitchen house. His handsome cheekbones make me forget about his bald head. He smiles all the time. It's as if with his happy-go-lucky ways he covers up his darker motivations. He is a natural flirt and, again, I notice Ling Li blush. I know she must fancy him, even when he tells us about his wife and children in Ipoh.

'Well, well, the guppy, and how is she?' he asks me.

'Quite well,' I answer in a funny made-up voice to sound like Ma'am. 'And you?'

'Things are going great. So, you going to join forces with me?' he asks.

'I'm in,' I say. 'I want to get rich and be my own Ma'am.'

'Well . . .' he laughs. 'Now we are talking. I knew you had some spirit.'

'Am I going to get rich?' I ask him. 'And . . . how does it work?' I ask.

'Well, we find a supply of helpers for agents who fill the new hotels and homes with maids, with women whose families pay us,' he says.

'Tell me more!' I ask him.

'It's called recruiting, I am looking and finding the best maids, but I need to have someone to help teach these girls. You know so much and could be the difference. We could be a great team, Mei Mei,' he says.

'After the baby,' says Ling Li.

'Don't make me wait!' says Mr Today.

Chapter Eighteen

ISABELLE GOH

1999

London

Detective, a new baby was something that the expat families treasured. In their minds was the hope that the empire could still grow and thrive here in the tropics. With every birth, they hang on to this misplaced belief.

That afternoon, we hear moaning and a call to us for warm water and towels, lots of them. Ma'am is in labour and will deliver. Sir stands guard; Cook, Ling Li, Suleiman, Vee, and I—we all sit together at the main table as the light grows dark, hoping for good news.

It is a long and difficult delivery—silence and occasional moaning and grunting, then silence. Ling Li is called to help, and the next morning, we hear the cry. Aunt Faith comes to tell us. A girl. She is to be called Rosamund. Rosie for short and she is healthy, but Ma'am is weak.

Over the days and weeks, I check in on this infant, hold her when asked. She has a bottom-heavy feel from the start, and tiny breast buds. She is a pink colour, then a bit yellow. She has a tuft of dark brown hair. I watch her toes furl and unfurl, her brow knot and reknot, and her bunched up fists find her face. Her eyes rarely stay open, but when she does open her eyes, she looks right into mine. I recognize her. Her eyes hold the same sheen in them as mine. Another Tiger girl. A baby like I've never seen before.

While the house celebrates this new life, the bone-break fever sleep erupts in the household. First Ma'am, then Sir, then I get it. I have terrifying dreams of birds building nests and someone breaking them apart. Birds are everywhere, on top of the water, in the air. Vee cools me down with wet towels. The bone-break fever sleep, that's what I call it. Dengue fever, mosquito borne. It is the first time, other than the time in hospital, that I rest. I haven't ever slept in, and even through my fever, I can sense the sound of routine all around me. There is so much work to do: the endless removal of stains from sheets, towels, underpants. My own bowels are loose and I can't move without everything aching. My head, my feet, my back, and my neck.

Ling Li brings me broth to sip on. I tuck my bedsheets around my head, shivering. I hope to die. But I don't, no one does and by the end of the dengue epidemic that surged through the household, it is Ma'am Tessa who looks the most ill. After birthing the baby and her fever, she has lost a lot of strength. She needs a cane for support or my own bony shoulders. Sir stays put, he travels less and I see them sit close together on the lawn in the evenings. He holds her hand, running his thumb over her knuckles and assures her in quiet tones that she will get better soon. The baby rarely cries and is loved, so loved. These weeks are a quiet time, a time of care and love and I feel happy.

The ceremony they call 'the christening' is held at St Andrew's Cathedral. Chiselled into marble slabs that hang on every wall are the names of the worshippers who died making the crossing from around the world to Singapore. I can read some of the names: there is Anna Sinclair, age four. Thomas Chatham, age two, young Master Charles Thompson. Then there are the dozens of names of dead boys and girls, men and women who died as a result of armed struggles. Wars fought in faraway lands and the more recent war.

I know I shouldn't, but in idle moments during the christening, I imagine Pash chasing me through the pews. He catches me and pulls my waist towards him, kissing me deeply. I take note of every detail about him, how his front teeth fold ever so slightly one over the other. The imaginary feel of his arm across my back, my neck in the fold of his shoulder, our weight, height, and breath meet and join, but only in my dreams.

The organ music begins and I am jolted out of my daydreaming. At the front of the cathedral, we rise. The wooden pews stretch with the bodies of people kneeling, sitting, and standing to pray and sing. I sing along, I remember this hymn, this song. The Jesus lady sang it to us when we lived with her. She would emphasize the last few words, the short staccato sounds punctuating the end, 'To Be a Pilgrim'. During the hymn, we hear a banging sound, of head against wood. Ma'am Tessa has fainted. The organist stops—there is a hush and Sir lies Ma'am down on the front pew. The organist restarts, and the congregation continues singing until Ma'am rises and stumbles confused towards the car.

The living room back at the house is full of tuberose and jasmine. The tea sets have all been polished, biscuits baked. There are baby gifts and cards all around the room. I am allowed to work in the main rooms as long as I stay mostly unseen. The scar above my lip is a thick line of hardening tissue and I cover my mouth often. I'm standing against the wall, wearing my best dress, my hair tied back. I am letting it grow to my waist. I have become thin, but my eyes are bright and watching. The Tiger girl is alive.

The women gather in the living room at the house nodding into their teacups, taking reassuring sips, clutching their saucers against their bosoms. 'Good health to Tessa,' the guests murmur. I keep my head lowered. I can tell the missionaries, the Jesus ladies, right away. They take too many pieces of cake, heap their spoons high with sugar and leave their soggy tea bags all around the living room for me to clean up. Their legs are scarred from untreated insect bites. As they cross and recross their ankles, scabs ooze pus into their sandal straps. 'God bless the child,' they say fluttering their eyelids heavenwards, revealing cloudy eyes, overburdened with tropical disease.

I had anticipated with great excitement what styles the ladies would be wearing, and watch in dismay as their curls wilt in the heat, giving off the smell of cheap hairspray. I notice Mrs Anne Zandstra sits apart from the group, her feet are kicked back behind her, the heel of her wooden shoe juts out like the shape of a kris. She holds onto her ordinary purse with both hands, twisting the bag into her lap. With her cropped hair and tiny gold stud earrings, she could pass as one of the missionaries. But I've heard she has money, her own family money.

The women all wait for Ma'am to appear. They concentrate on their napkins and smile without revealing their teeth. They lean towards each speaker, eager witnesses to any emerging scandal.

'Wonder if Tessa has fully recovered, you know dengue is no joke,' says one woman.

'She might be worried about help, getting a good amah, now that the courts, I mean this custody battle is a worry,' says another woman.

'Imagine, entrusting your child to another woman, then, this woman kidnaps your daughter?' whispers another.

'It's all a tragedy,' says another.

'That woman, what if she preys on another family?' says another.

'Did you hear? Adeline, the mother, went out three days after giving birth looking for Maria? She rode her bicycle all around the neighbourhood calling out for her Maria, but the Kempeitai rounded her up, her and all the other children,' says another.

'It's just too devastating,' says another.

'Shh, enough, this is time to celebrate. Come now, congratulations to Tessa and baby!' says Aunt Faith in a forced voice as Ma'am walks into the living room.

Following Ma'am is Vee, carrying the infant. The women peek at the baby. I lean my body in as well. The women coo and awe.

'What have you named her?' asks one woman.

'Rosamund Claire Arundel Hamilton,' says Aunt Faith triumphantly. 'She'll be called Rosie.'

'What a gorgeous name and beautiful baby!' the women mutter.

I overhear one woman mention Rosie's features.

'Who does she look like then?' asks Anne.

Ma'am stumbles forward and I reach for her arm to steady her. The women feign ignorance of the question asked, but then Anne Zandstra speaks again and everyone listens.

'Too early to tell, I'm sure. Congratulations, Tessa!' says Anne.

'You'll need extra hands to help you now,' says a woman trying to sound helpful.

'Speaking of help, I can't get anyone to work at the house, what with all this nonsense surrounding the Hertogh case,' says Anne.

'I know what you mean,' says another.

'Our one good maid got spooked by the unrest and went back to Johor and we are hosting them,' says Anne.

The women look down at their laps.

'Them?' Aunt Faith asks. 'As in Maria and Adeline?'

'Ja,' says Anne Zandstra.

'For how long?' continues Aunt Faith.

'A few days,' says Anne.

'Well, Mei Mei could go and help for a few days,' says Aunt Faith. 'Until you find what you need.'

'But Tessa needs help now, no?' asks Anne.

'We have two others. We'll be fine,' says Aunt Faith.

'Which one is she then, this Mei Mei?' asks Anne.

Aunt Faith points in my direction. I freeze. *No, I am not for show.* I look down. The leather straps on my sandals strain against my growing feet. My legs have grown leaner, my waist tighter. My cheekbones are more pronounced, my eyebrows arch in an angular way. My eyes, sometimes green, olive, light brown with gold flecks. The stain on my face is fading, but still a part of me.

'Mei Mei,' says Aunt Faith. 'Step forward girl.'

No, I can't be put on display like this, no.

'Come now. Don't be foolish. Mei Mei, stand up straight, so we can see you!' says Aunt Faith.

'Pity about her face, but she'll do,' says Anne Zandstra. 'She can start tomorrow morning.'

I am startled by this sudden turn of events, that I will be working at the Zandstras' and get a chance to meet Maria, the lost-and-found girl. I will need a new strength to tolerate this horrible man and a kindness to look out for Maria.

After the christening tea, Angus asks everyone to join him at the front of the house. He has hired a photographer to mark this occasion. Detective, it is like yesterday in my memory. Sir stands in the centre, to his left, next to him, is Ma'am. She is propped up by Aunt Faith. Next to Aunt Faith, Vee stands holding baby Rosie, I stand close by holding one hand over my mouth and the other hand holds onto Rosie's toes. To Sir's right stands Honour and Ling Li. Cook and Suleiman are placed at the back with Pash. Sir gathers the group together.

'I'd like to make a toast. To our dear Rosamund, welcome! Welcome baby Rosie to 24 Mount Rosie Road!' says Sir.

The crowd cheers and shares their congratulations with Ma'am and Sir for the new baby. Ma'am can barely stand and Vee and I help her back to her bed where she collapses and sleeps for days.

At the Zandstras', I finally see Maria's freckles up close. She is a minor celebrity, Detective, so imagine my surprise when she speaks to me. Maria is in the Zandstras' living room. The overstuffed sofa seems to envelop her frail figure. She holds a china tea cup in an exaggerated formal way and blows on the surface of the hot liquid. Her mother is in the front hall on a phone call. I heard Maria speaks Malay. I lean in towards her to pour her more tea.

'*Mahu makan?*' I whisper, asking her if she'd like to eat, not believing she is real.

'Ya, *saya lapar,*' she says.

The sound of her voice is so sad, it makes my knees wobble.

'Want anything special, to eat?' I ask her.

'Rambutan, have?' she asks, like her life depends on it.

I watch as Maria puts her tea cup down and fingers her kebaya. It is too big for her. She has folded over the sleeves. She looks like a girl pretending to be a woman, like she's in a rush to grow up.

'Let me check,' I tell her.

When I return from the kitchen with peeled mangosteen, Maria is sitting too close to Zandstra. He reaches out to twirl her curls in his thick fingers. I almost drop the plate.

'You can stay here for as long as you like,' says Zandstra to Maria.

'No rambutan, but I found these for you,' I interrupt.

Her fingers touch mine and I am surprised to feel they are cold. Zandstra stands up and moves towards Adeline, who has entered the room.

'*Terima kasih,*' she says.

Maria pops a segment of the fruit in her mouth and I do the same.

'I don't want to be here, and I don't want to go to Holland. I only want to stay with Aminah and Mansoor,' she tells me, her eyes filling with tears.

'I know,' I say.

'I am afraid,' she says. 'I don't want trouble.'

I find it in myself to speak more.

'Can I share something with you?'

'Ja,' she looks up with her wide eyes.

'Know who you are. Carry it in your heart. In your heart,' I tell her. My knowledge from the feng shui master, just the way he told me.

Chapter Nineteen

ISABELLE GOH

1999

London

Detective, I can't help myself. My imagination takes over and I imagine Rosie is mine. I imprint the feeling of her weight on my hip, her sweet head resting on my shoulder, her heaviness on my chest when she falls asleep. I tell myself that I would never, if I ever have my own children, have others care for them. I will be there every step, holding fast to my flesh and blood.

I strap her to my front in a sarong where she rests, her body bumps up against my chest as I do my housework. She falls asleep tied to my body, her sweaty brow and pink cheeks below my chin where I can blow on her forehead to cool her. Mine are the first eyes she meets when she wakes from sleep, my name is the first she utters when I come to wake her from her nap. She takes the bottle from me when Vee is called to help Ma'am. Ling Li tries, but she doesn't have the same patience she used to and so I become the default carer for this baby.

I wonder how Maria is doing at the Zandstras' and know that she would love a distraction from all the sadness and confusion. I wrap Rosie to my chest and walk her up to the Zandstras' home.

I know the way very well now. I anticipate the swell in the road, the vista of the jungle opening up at certain angles to allow a peek into the gardens of the neighbouring properties. Rosie snuggles in close as I walk to Malcolm Road. I have this feeling that she is mine, that she needs to be mine. *That's not right thinking*, I tell myself.

Maria loves Rosie. She sits, holding her carefully, cradling her little head. It is a dream to have Maria and Rosie together.

'She looks like you,' Maria tells me as Rosie looks up at her.

'You think so?' I ask.

'Yes, she is like you. Dark hair and light eyes,' says Maria. 'Mei Mei?'

'Yes, what is it?' I ask her.

'You need to take her away,' she says. 'Take Rosie, take her away from Zandstra and this place, it's not safe for any of us,' she says.

'I know,' I tell her.

Chapter Twenty

DETECTIVE AYESHA NUR

1999

London

When Zoe was placed on Ayesha's chest after the C-section, Ayesha's fingers still swollen from the drugs and the effort, she felt compelled to put Zoe to her breast immediately: to feed her, to nourish her. Ayesha was in love with Zoe, but her love very soon became tinged with extreme anxiety. Ayesha was so worried about her own thoughts, thoughts about harming her infant, but had no one to tell. Dom was out most nights and her own mother kept her distance from Ayesha's fear.

One night, holding Zoe in her arms, washing her limbs, Ayesha thought that it was not at all difficult to end Zoe's life. Ayesha started to have terrible thoughts. Ayesha guessed she was overtired and the emotions of all this new motherhood were overwhelming. Ayesha didn't ever harm Zoe. Once the dreadful feelings passed, and Zoe grew, Ayesha's love grew and now, Ayesha would die for her daughter, but she had to work on fighting back that panic, the feeling that she might never ever really love Zoe the way she is supposed to.

Chapter Twenty-One

MEI MEI

1950

Singapore

As much as I can care for Rosie on my own, I am still a child myself. I am overworked and get distracted.

'Mei Mei!' cries Ling Li from the terrace. 'Mei Mei!'

I jump up from where I've been lying on the floor.

'Yes. What? Here, what?' I say.

'Where's, where's the baby? Where is she?' demands Ling Li.

'Rosie?' I rub my eyes.

'Get up, stupid girl, get up!' screams Ling Li.

What have I done? Where is she? She was lying on a blanket in front of me just a minute ago. Vee had asked me to watch her while she sent a message to Suleiman. I remember watching her lying on the blanket on the cool tiles of the veranda, right in front of me. I must have fallen asleep.

'She's gone, come on, get up!' yells Ling Li.

My heart is racing. She couldn't have gotten very far. No, Zandstra, no! No, I can't even imagine him holding her. I sniff the air like an animal for the telltale sign of his cologne and stink.

I search, hunting for signs of danger and hear the sound of gentle laughter. I look out towards the edge of the garden.

'Pash? Pash, is that you?' I ask.

I run outside onto the grass. He is standing under the casuarina tree holding baby Rosie.

'Yes, we're here,' he says calmly.

'Rosie!' I run to her and reach for her. 'Thank God!'

'You fell asleep, I picked her up. We are on a tour of the gardens! Right, Rosie?' he says.

'Ling Li! I found her, she's here!' I yell back towards the house.

'It's all right, Mei Mei. Rosie is fine. You fell asleep, it's all fine, I would never let any harm come to her. None of us would,' says Pash.

'Thank you,' I say.

'It's nothing, she's such a good girl, aren't you?' asks Pash playfully.

'Thank you, thank you,' I repeat shaking.

'Calm yourself, everything is all right,' says Pash.

'She's just so innocent and Zandstra . . . he . . .' I begin.

'What's it like then?' he asks.

'What's what like?' I ask him back.

'The Zandstras?' he asks.

'I hate it, I hate him,' I blurt out. 'Sorry, but I do, what he does,' I say.

'What does he do now?' asks Pash.

'He finds other people, other maids and the male servants, he takes anyone. He wants everyone and he's so ugly,' I say.

Pash's expression changes from being playful to being dead serious.

'He's pushed us all down. We need to protect Rosie from him, he can never have her,' says Pash.

'I agree, but how, how do we prevent him? He is . . .' I say.

'Think, think, you are a clever girl, when you go there to visit with Maria, look for ways, ways we can stop him,' he says with such great urgency that it scares me.

I feel so much love for Pash. He is my hero, my knight in shining armour. I laugh. *That would make me his sleeping beauty*. I am awake, more than I've ever been. And with a mission to stop the evil Zandstra from getting hold of our precious baby.

It has become very hot again and I am inside the main house cleaning the stairwell when I see Honour at the top of the stairs. She looks listless and is sucking the ends of her hair. Master Tong is right again, she looks exhausted. Her eyes are colourless and her skin is pale.

'I know all about you two,' I tell her.

'You know nothing,' says Honour.

'You'd best be very careful. He's a good person, you don't want him to get into trouble.'

'Back off,' says Honour. 'What would you know?'

'More than you think,' I say. 'Everyone knows you go together, you need to be careful.'

'Why would you even care?' asks Honour.

'People always watching and your reputation,' I tell her.

'What does that matter, I'm in love, we're in love,' she says.

I feel sick and angry, all mixed together, but swallow this feeling.

'You remember when I worked at the Zandstras'?' I say.

'Ja,' says Honour.

'They are going away soon with Maria and Adeline. I can speak to their maid, and you could have the house to yourselves for a night. I know where they keep all the keys to the rooms,' I share.

'You, you would do that for me, for us?' she asks.

'Of course,' I lie.

'Why? Why would you do this?' she asks.

'Someone deserves to be happy,' I reply.

Such lovesick fools. I lick the scar above my lip. I am amazed at how easy it is to lie. I have wriggled my way into their love story. Trying to find some sort of sick power over them.

What I haven't factored in, though, is Zandstra's true nature. No one expects them to come home earlier and once Zandstra sees Pash with Honour, Zandstra wants to have her for himself. Zandstra wants both of them. My pathetic attempt at revenge only leads to a much worse outcome.

Chapter Twenty-Two

MEI MEI

1950

Singapore

I don't think any of us expected to be so captivated by Rosie, this small child. She is just the sweetest of angels. She brings everyone together. Aunt Faith is besotted, she dotes on Rosie and wants to teach us all a song to sing for her.

'Teach it to Mei Mei! Teach it to Mei Mei!' says Vee.

'Mei Mei can't sing! And, Vee, you are too sharp!' says Aunt Faith.

'How do you know Mei Mei can't sing?' asks Vee.

'With a mouth like that, not likely,' says Aunt Faith.

'Let's see, maybe she has a sweet voice,' says Vee.

'Oh, all right then,' says Aunt Faith.

Aunt Faith teaches me a lullaby. Vee and Ling Li know the phrase. It is a round. We need four voices. Aunt Faith starts and each of us copy the notes, entering at different places. This sound of our voices joining, circling, repeating is the church bells I have heard in town some days. To me, this is the sound of completeness, of charmed beauty. My voice is not what you'd expect coming out of those crooked teeth and the lumpy mound over my split lip.

It is a searching voice. It yearns and longs for connection and harmony. And Vee's voice has a soothing timbre that makes you feel that everything is right with the world.

Aunt Faith starts the lullaby, Vee follows, then Ling Li. I sing the song without really understanding a word, but it isn't the words we need, just the sound of our voices fitting together. The melody repeats and naturally harmonizes, and our voices lift our spirits.

Matthew, Mark, Luke, and John,
Bless this bed that I lie on.
Four corners to my bed,
Four angels round my head;
One to watch and one to pray
And two to bear my sins away.

Our voices combine to find the spaces between the notes and fill them with beauty. We sing the round over and over in turns like a wheel turning round and round. Aunt Faith, Ling Li, Vee, and I, singing to Rosie. I feel a warmth in my heart and a sense of what belonging to a family feels like. These sounds have colour, and with the love I feel, it is overwhelming. I see warm hues of eggplant purple and it feels like the silk blouse I wash for Ma'am after I've ironed it and it falls in perfect folds on a hanger.

I love Rosie. She doesn't mind my crooked mouth or the stain on my face. I hold her, burp her, walk her, soothe her, let her cry a little—it is a talent I have, I can comfort her. I dedicate myself to taking her everywhere with me.

That night, after soothing Rosie to sleep with the song, the winds from the northeast bring a change all around the island. High winds and a rare coolness. The winds bring insects. They build hives and the sun rarely shines. The air is close and even with deep breaths, my lungs feel like they can't fill up with new air. Rosie has become a little restless and hot to the touch.

'Mei Mei! Wake up! It's the baby. She can't stop crying . . . you must come, now,' says Ling Li.

I climb out of my cot and up the backstairs, following Rosie's cries. I hold out my arms and coo for her, she reaches her little arms for me and I walk her around the room. She is burning with a fever.

'Shshsh, there, there, all okay, Mei Mei is here with you, shh,' I calm her.

I stay with her all night, pressing damp cloths on her back and her belly, keeping her cool. While Ma'am sleeps, I walk and hold her baby. Baby Rosie.

By morning, the fever has broken and Rosie rests. Ling Li takes over watching her and I walk towards the back of the garden, trying to clear my head and offer up thanks for Rosie's good health. But there on the ground on the stone path in front of me, I find three dead embryos. I remember Ling Li telling me the koel invades the nests of other birds, disguises their eggs to look like the host birds' eggs, then when the host birds' eggs hatch, the koel chicks push the other chicks out of the nest when they are born. I stare too long at the birds with their unformed bodies and feel afraid of my own thoughts. I hang on to that vision of death for too long before I collapse on my cot for a long sleep.

I am up on the second floor, cleaning the window panes that line the side of the house overlooking the swimming pool, one hundred and forty-four windows in total, when I see Zandstra walking alongside the pool. Honour is swimming, unaware that he is stalking her. From where I am, I can see him approach the edge of the pool and grab Honour. I drop the pail I am holding and keep watching. Honour must think it's a game as I hear her laughing—or is she shouting? I open the windows and see her swimming for her life to the opposite end of the pool. She pulls herself out and races across the garden up the slight incline and into the house. I leave my cleaning and head down the back stairs and into the kitchen house. She is standing soaking wet in the middle of the servants' quarters.

'Help me. Hide me!' she says.

Her legs and feet are covered in red mud, her wet hair hangs in front of her face and she can barely catch her breath. In that moment, I make a decision. Do I help her, the person who harmed me, who pushed me? I don't want to, I want her to suffer, but we need to band together if we are going to stay safe.

'In here,' I tell her. 'Hide, hide, under my cot. No one will come in here,' I tell her.

I watch through my small window as Zandstra reaches the servants' quarters. His normal, ruddy countenance is enhanced by his exertion and all the whiskey. We can smell him.

'Honour! I know you're here. Honour!' he calls.

He is grunting like a wild boar. He is huffing. He pulls at the tufts of his orange hair and wipes his forehead with a yellow-stained handkerchief. He sounds angry and desperate.

'Where are you? I'll find you!' he yells.

'Sir,' says Cook respectfully.

'Out of my way! Water!' he demands. 'A glass of water!'

Ling Li leaves a glass on the table that he downs. He continues his rampage, calling for Honour.

'I know you're in here, come out!' he demands.

'Please no, please, no,' whispers Honour under my cot.

'Just wait, he will leave soon,' I tell her.

Honour is silent. We hear Zandstra walking back and forth, calling out her name in between roars of outrage, and then he leaves for the main house.

'There, there, he is gone now, there, there,' I tell her.

She slowly crawls out from under my cot and I get her a sarong to cover herself.

'I'm not safe in the house,' she tells me.

'You can stay here, with me and Ling Li,' I say.

'Where will I sleep?' she asks.

'Here, with me,' I say.

'Why would I trust you?' she asks.

'Who else is going to help you?' I ask.

I bring her dinner. She won't go back to the house. I sit with her on my cot.

'We have to stop Zandstra,' she says.

'I have some ideas, but we will need to work together,' I say. 'We need Pash's help.'

Honour is still shivering from the close call. Zandstra is still out there. We can sense he is in the main house. Then I hear Rosie. She is crying. I need to find out what she needs.

'Stay here,' I tell Honour.

I walk across the walkway and see Zandstra holding Rosie. She is screaming. Zandstra is forcing her to lie still in his arms. I hear Ma'am's sing-song voice and then more crying. Vee is standing at the ready to take Rosie. I can see Pash retrieving his bicycle from the side of the house. I walk towards him.

'Pash, we need you,' I tell him, quietly.

'What?' he asks.

'We need to find a way to stop Zandstra,' I say with an urgency that comes straight from my heart.

After Zandstra has left staggering along the laneway out to Malcolm Road, I imagine a way. Pash, Honour, and I sit on the steps of the kitchen house and as dusk turns to darkness, the three of us concoct a plan. It doesn't matter how we will do it, all we know is that we have to stop Zandstra and that we need to end it. His life.

Part III

RAGE

Chapter Twenty-Three

MEI MEI

1950

Singapore

Sir, Zandstra, and a number of other men are in the living room, talking about Maria. Maria. Her name sounds like a possibility up in the clouds, like an exultation. I am tasked with emptying out ashtrays and I overhear them talk. One man is athletic and light on his feet, twitchy like a dog needing to run. His name is Matthews. Another is a man named Fellowes. He moves slowly and smells like onions.

'Why aren't the British getting involved?' asks Zandstra.

'Oh, but we are,' answers Sir.

'How so?' asks Zandstra.

'The trial is to be played out in the British courts, with a British judge and lawyers. I don't see the Dutch leading along legal grounds,' says Sir.

I try to make out what the men are talking about. It seems even the white men can't agree on this topic of Maria. I don't understand why there is so much argument around a girl, such a kind, sweet child.

'The Dutch? We are long gone in this region,' says Zandstra. 'And you British, you never made any real money here, so utterly ignorant, you relied on the Peranakans for everything. This trial is all just a last-ditch effort at trying to take back what little control you never had.'

'Then why are you still here, Zandstra?' asks Matthews.

'Nowhere else to be. In that way I am like Maria, I guess,' says Zandstra. 'Another poor Dutch bastard.'

The men lean in and then out with their laughter. Their yellow teeth are pointed. They remind me of wild dogs.

'The Dutch have no clear role here, but we do need to ensure this girl goes home,' says Zandstra.

'Home? And where is home to *you*, Zandstra? Your family goes back generations in Asia,' says Matthews.

The man named Fellowes gets up from his chair slowly and stands looking out of the veranda doors at the garden.

'Home? No idea about that, but what I do know is no Dutch girl should be raised Muslim—the facts are she was stolen from her family. Stolen, and she needs to go back,' says Zandstra.

I see Zandstra suck in his cheeks and pour himself another whiskey.

'I say we should leave it as a family matter, would you not agree? I mean, how is it really our concern?' asks Fellowes.

'Family? It has gone beyond a family matter now, it was always a political story from the get-go,' says Matthews. 'It's humanity's concern.'

'Steady on,' says Fellowes.

'Steady on? Have we not learned anything from the war? The tensions rise up and . . .' begins Matthews.

'And we need to let them rise, they'll subside eventually, it's just the natural course of things,' says Fellowes

'Wonder what Lim would make of all this?' asks Matthews. 'I mean it's brilliant, keeps us all divided. The whole system is in their favour now.'

'They've set up a system just the way we did, elite schools feed into elite roles. Everyone else left scrambling. Can't you see what this really means? It means we're tribal,' says Matthews.

'True enough. This region will be hard to control, though, too many competing interests, too little space,' says Fellowes.

'It does feel a bit tense lately. The press business doesn't help. The local presses have stirred this up even further pitting Christendom against Islam!' says Matthews.

'Oh, and where do you think they get their ideas from? The European press have been disgraceful—leave the young girl alone. Let her decide where she wants to live, what she wants to believe in, who she wants to love,' says Sir.

'The minute we give in to them, it's all over,' says Zandstra.

'What's all over, Zandstra?' asks Sir.

'European dominance,' says Zandstra slurring his words.

'God, man, you, you just said it yourself, that's been over for decades. Our time is well up. Nobody wanted us here in the first place, and what with the communists hiding out in Malaya, it's time we left for good,' says Fellowes.

The feeling I sense from these men is disappointment, disappointment in themselves, in their empire, in the choices they've made. The men thank Sir for the evening. Matthews and Fellowes wait for their drivers while Zandstra sways into the night along the length of the driveway and up to Malcolm Drive to his own domain, where his staff cower in the shadows and hold their breath until his light goes out beside his bed.

The servants stay quiet about Maria at first. It is the English making such a big deal of Maria, but I sense this is all getting bigger, much bigger than all of us. I believe all of this is about freedom. Other groups join in the protests and a power base grows, furthering their reasons to dislodge the British power in the region, they see

Maria as their rallying cry to get even. Maria's case is everyone's business. Maria's story becomes everyone's story.

At first, it is mainly the two camps jostling for position. The young Muslim men feel personally insulted that the religion of a girl who chose Islam, and was married to a Muslim, is not recognized. The Muslims feel dishonoured, and the newspaper men rile up the crowd.

I want so very much to believe that Maria's mother wants the best for Maria, but it is all so confusing. No one is letting the women talk. What really happened that fateful day? Did Adeline give Maria away? Did Che Aminah understand it differently? Did a child's future not factor in? I remember the story Ling Li told me about the koel, that some mothers in nature disguise their eggs to be raised in another nest by a different bird. Perhaps Adeline did this. My imagination takes over and I see Maria's mother as the koel, placing her daughter into the care of another bird, Che Aminah, who could take better care.

The kitchen house is fragmented into feelings and allegiances. If the kitchen house is split and so is the main house, then the whole island, the region, and the world must also be experiencing a serious case of misunderstanding. Vee is on Maria's side, so am I. Maria has nothing to do with the politics. Her own voice is never heard.

I can feel that all of us are worried about the future. When I think about the word 'worry', I see a pattern, not so much a colour. This whole situation affects my way of seeing and my vision becomes blurry. It's like I can see holes, like polka dots, letting in light like mother of pearl, shimmering across my field of vision, impacting everything I see. It is distracting.

The English seem to have regained some power in the courts, in the law making, and Cook tells me quietly that the English masters are afraid of the communists threatening the labour groups. His brothers hiding out in the jungles of Malaysia are another growing voice of dissatisfaction. All of us are afraid.

On top of all this, Ma'am is not getting better. She can't eat and vomits most days. Her fever isn't responding to any of the medication the doctor brings. The night she has a seizure, Sir is convinced she needs hospital treatment, but the roads are becoming unsafe and no doctor will come to house during the tension, no one will risk their own safety. Not now, not here.

Chapter Twenty-Four

DETECTIVE AYESHA NUR

1999

London

The interviews with Isabelle are exhausting and it's been her week with Zoe. Ayesha is amazed at how Zoe is growing. Her chubby cheeks are giving way to angled cheekbones, an elongated chin, and where her neck was thick and short, it is now lengthening, giving her extra height. Zoe is twelve going on thirteen, a child turning into a young woman. Ayesha wants to hold onto her, curl her arm around her daughter's waist, draw her in close, etch this feeling of her soft embrace forever on her heart, but her own stress prevents her from reaching for her own child.

Ayesha walks down the hallway of her flat and knocks on her daughter's bedroom door. Zoe is sitting with her back to the door wearing headphones. Ayesha taps Zoe on her shoulder.

'How about a movie, kid?' asks Ayesha.

'Whatever,' says Zoe.

'Your choice, I'm fine with whatever you'd like,' says Ayesha.

'You know we can never decide on what to watch,' says Zoe.

Ayesha doesn't want to overthink it, but she feels her daughter's words like a sharp backslap. Ayesha is looking up movie showtimes when her phone rings.

'Chief, Archer is gone,' says Steve.

'Who, what?' asks Ayesha.

'Commissioner Archer, she's resigned. Off the books! We can keep going, keep the hunt, the chase, on,' says Steve.

'I never gave up,' says Ayesha.

'Me neither,' says Steve.

'Who's on it? I mean who's in charge, who's on it?' demands Ayesha.

'Yan, Pamela Yan. Ever heard of her?' asks Steve.

'No, new to me,' says Ayesha.

'My contacts tell me she's good. Did time in counterterrorism,' says Steve.

'Whoa, impressive. We need to keep our heads down, keep moving forward, no mistakes. Time to bring in Bishop Roy. All of this has to be handled with kid gloves or it's our necks on the line. Yours and mine,' says Ayesha to Steve.

'We're back on, boss!' says Steve.

Ayesha ends the call and smiles. She turns to Zoe and ruffles the hair on her daughter's head.

'Sorry about that, darling,' says Ayesha.

'Who was that?' asks Zoe.

'Work,' says Ayesha. 'I know, it never ends . . . come on, let's catch that movie.'

'It's too late now, I'm tired,' says Zoe.

Ayesha is torn between the rush her job gives her, the feeling of being alive, and the feeling of never being able to get anything right with Zoe.

'What if I ordered a pizza, would that work?' asks Ayesha.

'I guess that would work,' mumbles Zoe.

Bishop Roy needs no introduction, but he does require discretion. He arrives wearing plain clothes, no purple robes. He looks good. Handsome, fit, and well-mannered.

'Very good to meet you both,' says Bishop Roy.

He bows his head respectfully towards Ayesha and Steve as he takes a seat at the table across from them.

'Thank you for your time, Bishop,' says Steve.

Ayesha notices Bishop Roy's eye muscles tense as he presses his lips closed.

'Please, Pash is fine, please just call me Pash,' he says.

Ayesha and Steve let out a joint breath of relief and share nervous laughter.

'As you know, we are interviewing those who knew the victim of a recent attempted homicide, in St James's Place,' says Ayesha.

'Yes, I am aware. My wife told me. We knew her, we knew Mei Mei, when we were young,' says Pash.

Ayesha is impressed that he is to the point, no beating about the bush.

'What can you tell us about Isabelle? When did you see her last?' asks Steve.

Pash looks off, past their heads, like he's trying to recall a memory.

'The last time you saw her. Isabelle, Isabelle Goh?' asks Ayesha.

'Yes, right, we last saw each other professionally,' says Pash.

'Come again?' asks Steve. 'How do you mean?'

'At the cathedral,' says Pash.

Pash wipes his palms on his jeans, and reaches for a glass of water on the table.

'Are you saying that Isabelle Goh came to St Paul's, to the cathedral?' asks Ayesha.

'Yes,' says Pash. 'I spoke with her on occasion after services. I mean we have vast crowds in the congregation, a lucky problem to have. She made herself known to me and we talked. She had many enemies. I mean, none of us are perfect,' says Pash.

'And the last time you saw her?' asks Steve.

'November 12,' says Pash.

'The day someone tried to kill her,' says Ayesha.

'Yes,' says Pash.

'Why would anyone want her dead?' asks Steve.

Pash removes his glasses, pinches the space at the top of the bridge of his nose and replaces his glasses, blinking.

'What do you make of the attempt on her life?' asks Ayesha.

'May I have more water?' asks Pash.

'Certainly,' says Ayesha and refills his glass from the water cooler.

Pash drains the glass and clears his throat.

'I think the lies were catching up to her, to all of us,' says Pash.

'Lies, what lies?' asks Ayesha.

'All of us, we all have layers of identities,' says Pash.

'Indeed, what about her lies gives you the impression someone wanted to end her life?' asks Ayesha.

'It's a long story, complicated. I don't know how much my wife shared with you, what Honour shared with you, but . . .' says Pash. 'We did this to protect Rosie,' says Pash.

'You did what? Please tell us more, this Rosie, where can we find her?' says Ayesha.

'None of us know any more. We cared for her until she was old enough to care for herself,' says Pash.

Pash's voice cracks and he reaches again for the water. With both hands, he lifts the bottle up and drinks. His hands shake slightly.

'We felt a shared desire to protect Rosie from a man . . . Pieter Zandstra,' says Pash.

Pash draws in a deep breath. He brings his hands together as if in prayer and lifts them to his face. His fingers touch his lips and he lets out a short, sharp breath.

'Do you need a minute?' asks Ayesha.

'No, I'm all right. I've just never told anyone about Zandstra. He was a terrible man from our childhood. I . . . I'm so sorry. It's inappropriate of me, I shouldn't be speaking like this,' says Pash.

'We all have our own opinions. Please, continue,' says Steve.

'Yes, but the difference is, and it's a big one, I have been trained to love, to love the sinner,' says Pash.

'We all have these kinds of thoughts, Pash,' says Steve.

'Yes, but I was trained *not* to have these,' says Pash. 'So that makes me even more despicable.'

'Bishop . . . Pash, please,' says Ayesha. 'Let's stick with the facts. You saw Mei Mei the night of her attempted murder, correct? Did you speak with her?'

'Yes, I've told you.' says Pash. 'I mean, it's been so long since I thought of all this, I was only a teenager, so young.'

'When you what, Sir? So young, Sir?' asks Steve.

'I was working at the house on Mount Rosie Road just on Sundays, initially, I was considering the path to being an ordained priest in the Anglican Church of Singapore,' says Bishop Roy.

'I see,' says Steve.

'At the house on Mount Rosie Road, my aunt Vee, Suleiman, all of us knew Isabelle. We knew her as Mei Mei back then,' says Pash.

'Yes,' says Steve.

'Mei Mei, she was an odd one, she was always following us around, she must have been a very lonely young thing, not many other children around, just Honour . . . and me on Sundays. And I wasn't paying much attention. I had become obsessed with prayer. My knees were all calloused, I'd been praying for Zandstra to leave me alone, but my real prayer was to be close to . . . to Honour,' says Pash.

'Carry on,' says Ayesha.

'We became friends, the three of us. It was us against him,' says Pash.

'Him?' asks Steve.

'Zandstra,' says Pash.

'He had his way with Ma'am, with me, with Honour, and we were terrified that Rosie would be a victim. He had an insatiable appetite, a sexual appetite,' says Pash coughing nervously. 'And so, yes, we did take matters into our own hands, but we had no other way to protect ourselves, our world was . . .' says Pash. 'But that's behind us now.'

'Is there something more you need to share with the police, Pash?' asks Ayesha.

'No, that's all over,' says Pash.

'And Isabelle's attempted murder, her association with the underworld, what can you tell us about that?' asks Steve.

'Like I said, we all have enemies,' says Pash. 'Her enemies had more to lose, she got too close to some bad people. If that is all, I really must end this here. Many duties to fulfil, as you can imagine.'

'Bishop Edward Roy, do not leave London, if we need to interview you again, will be in touch,' says Ayesha.

'I understand,' says Pash.

Chapter Twenty-Five

MEI MEI

December 1950

Singapore

That December, the days were particularly rainy and dark clouds seized the sky. By early evening, the servants' quarters were very gloomy. I could sense that all the characters in the house were nervous, there was unresolved tension in the air.

'There is a large crowd gathering in the city, near the *padang*,' says Sir.

All of us servants are gathered in the kitchen.

'Is it about that girl, Maria, Sir?' asks Cook.

'Yes, Liu,' says Sir.

'Anybody hurt, Sir?' asks Suleiman.

'We will know more in the morning. Please . . .' says Sir.

Vee reaches for my hand. Ling Li pulls her apron strings around to the front of her waist and worries at them. Cook and Suleiman shuffle.

'No one goes outside the gates. Until I say. Understand?' says Sir.

'Yes, Sir,' we respond.

'Let this whole situation calm down,' says Sir.

'Yes, Sir,' we say.

It all seems so far away from our reality. We can't hear any of the raised voices from the crowds or see placards lifted high. And yet I can sense a restlessness in the air as if someone has filled a balloon with too much hot air. The aftermath of the war has left dry hearts everywhere, there was no time to heal and now this new hostility is stoking an invisible fire. It is high drama on all sides.

I will remember the next three days like they were yesterday. I am too young to recollect the fear the Japanese invaders caused, although Ling Li reminds me. Here, in the house, I am being pulled in different directions, told to side with different factions, with Liu and his brothers waiting in the bush to take down the whole system, with Honour and Aunt Faith to face reason and rationality, and then with Vee and Pash who just want Maria to have a fair outcome. Suleiman sides with Che Aminah. Ling Li just wants for all this to blow over, for people to come to their right minds. There is a pitting of allegiances in so many directions.

The court's decisions are explained in the paper, and each day it seems like someone else has custody of Maria. First Che Aminah, then the courts, then the children's aid society, and then Maria's own family. The situation is heartbreaking. It is a family affair that has overnight become a one-sided war of rage. At its centre is a misunderstanding, overlaid with the people's fear of a directionless future.

And they say that we shouldn't talk about it, about how rising tensions between racial groups can rise, but this is the true reality: humanity's ugly head is always inches away from destruction, like Vee said, 'We are all slightly angry most of the time.' And I am here. *I* am. Mei Mei, me, I am here.

On the first night, I am holding Rosie, waiting for the all-clear to bring her in to say goodnight to her parents when I overhear Ma'am and Sir talking.

'The thugs are attacking anyone who wants Maria to go back to Holland,' says Ma'am. 'But the courts already gave custody to Che Aminah.'

'Until the full force of the law comes down on the Hertogh side,' says Sir.

'So then why this threat of violence?' asks Ma'am.

'This is getting bigger and bigger by the day,' says Sir.

'I've heard the press continue to stir things up,' says Ma'am. 'I mean whose idea was it to let the journalists and photographers into the convent? This is a private matter, between a family and a guardian.'

'Well, it's a global issue now, great offense has been taken to the court's decision,' says Sir. 'And there is money at stake now, money coming in to support the cause.'

'There's a cause?' asks Ma'am.

'This is a pressure cooker. Steam will need to be released. The facts are: a Christian court is determining the fate of a Muslim girl, there's no way anyone will win,' says Sir.

'Ja, a girl who was married off as a minor without consultation with her parents,' says Ma'am.

'. . . who is a Dutch citizen and christened into the Roman Catholic Church,' says Sir.

'She is Eurasian, her mother was half Malay,' says Ma'am.

'In the eyes of the court, she is a white child,' says Sir.

Their words are fast and animated, but there is a feeling of dread underneath their words, like no one will win. I imagine a sea of blue grey with waves pulling back in leaving black sludge along the floor of the sea, writhing with ugly sea creatures, their tentacles reaching up and out. I shake my head to clear the image away. It is too real.

The second day is worse; the crowds surrounding Che Aminah and Maria, the two of them being torn apart. We can't look away. The images of Maria being pulled away from the arms of Che Aminah and how the crowds surge around her, open up her pain to our own. I see a wave of injustice brought home on a girl's face. This one image in the newspaper makes me feel ashamed of all of us.

It is heart-wrenching. Maria only having known Che Aminah as a loving caregiver is being taken from her. Maria is forced away from her new husband and a loving community to live with her mother who has flown in from Holland while the colonial judges make the final decision: Maria is to go back to be with her family, in a country she has never known. And then, when the first gunshots are fired, the crowds are three thousand strong. They push and shove and that's when I solidify my plan. I can make use of this, this chaos.

It rained in the morning before sunrise. There is a steady breeze in the tops of the trees fanning out and down to where I stand in the front hall with Honour. Ma'am has had another seizure and Sir is desperate to get her medical care. Sir walks Ma'am down the stairs and Honour and I help her into the car. Honour and I sit in the back seat on either side of Ma'am. Aunt Faith waves to us from inside the front hall. Vee stands at the front steps holding Rosie. Before we drive off, Rosie calls out my name and my heart warms.

The roads are blocked. Suleiman drives. Sir is up front. I sit in the back with Ma'am and Honour. The day turns bright and dry with a light breeze, a perfect laundry day. We wind ourselves down towards the bottom of Chancery Lane and pass youth marching towards the city holding up banners—'Justice for Maria', reads one; 'Justice for Mansoor', reads another; 'Che Aminah speaks the truth', says yet another. They shout out '*Nadra! Nadra!*' And '*Allahu Akbar!*'

'Angus, should we be on the roads?' mumbles Ma'am. 'Let's turn back.'

She coughs and I can see it pains her. I make myself small in the car. Suleiman holds on tightly to the steering wheel and looks ahead without blinking.

'Zandstra warned us of trouble,' says Ma'am.

'Zandstra did, did he? What would that fool know about trouble,' says Sir.

I haven't seen Sir speak in this tone to Ma'am before, he seems tired and annoyed.

'Just as long as the ports are safe, no violence at the ports and we'll be fine,' says Sir.

'The ports, that's what you're thinking about at a time like this?' says Ma'am.

'Directly to the front doors of the Bowyer Block, please, Suleiman. Mei Mei, you take care of Ma'am. Honour, we'll drop you with Ms Griffith-Jones,' says Sir.

As we turn onto Beach Road a large crowd is growing, and they surround the car. It all happens so fast. First, they drag Sir out. I tell myself to remain calm.

'Routine checkpoint, Ma'am,' says Suleiman.

Ma'am opens the car door and gets out of the car to follow Sir. Suleiman follows Ma'am. The madness begins. Suleiman is immediately hit on the head with a bat and falls, his head knocks against the car door where I am sitting. Honour starts screaming. I slip under the front passenger seat.

I hear Suleiman groaning and open the car door and pull him inside the vehicle to protect him from further beatings. He is calling out for his wife and daughter. I hear a sound in the distance, the sound of a bat smashing skulls, hands, bones breaking. It is a sickening sound and I want to vomit. I pull myself up in the seat and Honour and I watch the whole scene unfold. We see Ma'am pushed to the ground. Sir is being dragged further and further away. A man is beating Ma'am's legs—she has given up screaming.

The masses continue to file around the stopped car, looking for another body to harm.

'Sister, ang moh have? In car?' asks a young man.

'No one here, no, lah,' I say as I push Honour under the front seat ahead of me.

After the man passes, Honour puts her hand on the car door frame, looking out to find where her aunt and uncle are, and as the crowd passes, a man lifts up his bat and smashes it down on Honour's left hand. She screams in terror. Her left hand is broken, smashed. Honour folds into herself and clutches her arm screaming. I get out of the car to look for Ma'am and Sir. I find Ma'am, her face is covered in blood. I drag her to the car. I see she has lost consciousness. Honour stays with Ma'am near the car and I go in search of Sir.

'Sir, Sir?' I call out, but the crowd is chanting, 'Nadra! Justice for Nadra!' My voice is drowned out by the crowd.

I find him. He is lying face down in a drain. He is badly beaten and not breathing. I feel sick and terrified. A man comes over to me. He looks like Mr Lim. It is Mr Lim.

'This is Angus Sir, Hamilton Sir,' I yell. 'Please help me.'

Mr Lim helps me lift Sir's broken body and we drag him into the car. Mr Lim jumps in and drives us all to the hospital.

There are very few words that I have as a child to describe the heart of blackness I witness, where young men beating others spur on even greater violence, just for the sake of it, with no real understanding of the complexities of people who care for one another, for the innocent who are caught up in a political game and a misunderstanding, this great misunderstanding between two women about a girl.

As we arrive at the hospital, Mr Lim says he will find Aunt Faith. I am so traumatized that I can't register what he is saying to me. I feel like my internal organs are seeping out of my body. Sir's death is confirmed in the emergency room. It is a routine pronouncement but I am devastated. I want to slow down time, to stop the movement of people all around me in the hospital. I want to go back and reverse what has just happened, to prevent Sir from leaving the vehicle, to prevent Ma'am ever getting sick, but there is more desperation to come and I am needed.

Suleiman is bleeding profusely from his head wound. I walk him to a chair and sit while orderlies place Ma'am on a stretcher and she is given a hospital bed. Honour is taken to another room where her injury is treated. I sit for hours with Suleiman until he is finally seen. I pace the halls, not knowing what to do, who to turn to. After what seem like days, I ask a nurse about Ma'am and find myself in a room. Aunt Faith stands guard with her niece.

'What hell, what hell is this, what a nightmare! Where is Honour? Lim tells me the crowd was violent,' says Aunt Faith.

'Ma'am Faith?' I say. 'Ma'am?'

'What is it?' she asks.

'Angus Sir, he's . . . dead,' I say.

As I say this, the world stops for a moment. Our Sir, Angus, the one man who showed humanity, no more. Aunt Faith stumbles backwards into the wall and I hear a slow wail coming from Ma'am.

'No, no, this can't be happening. Where is Honour?' asks Aunt Faith.

'Getting treatment,' I say. 'Where is Rosie, is she safe?'

'Yes, she is, she is, thank God,' she says.

Ma'am's hospital room feels too warm, the air smells like wet blood, like death. I look at Ma'am's head, she has bandages across her forehead. I move closer to the edge of her bed.

'Mei Mei, I have been . . .' I hear her say.

I shift in the chair.

'It's all right, rest, Ma'am,' I say.

'I have been a terrible . . . Will you?' she tries again.

'Ma'am, it is time for you to rest, to heal,' I tell her.

'I'm not healing, I'm . . . dying,' says Ma'am.

'I pray for you. I get Pash?' I ask. 'He knows about the church.'

'Too late,' says Ma'am.

'If you can find him, please bring him here,' says Aunt Faith.

I step into the hall and find a way to Pash. Along the hospital corridors, past the wards, the smell of burned skin, of antiseptic, I make my way to the front doors, but the roads are not safe. Then I see him walking towards the Bowyer Block, under the covered walkway.

'Pash! Pash!' I scream out for him.

'Mei Mei! You all right?' he asks.

'Yes,' I say.

He grabs my arm.

'Ling Li, she told me to come. Sir, Ma'am, where's Honour?' he asks.

'Sir, Sir is dead. Ma'am very sick. Suleiman badly injured. Honour, Honour will be all right,' I say.

I can't believe I'm actually saying these words and Pash keeps shaking his head vigorously.

'What? Sir dead? How? Where are they?' he asks.

'Ma'am is this way, come.' I show him the way.

Pash arrives in Ma'am's room. Aunt Faith makes way for him to come to the bedside. His presence in the room brings a calmness and a fresh scent in the air like new rain.

'You are in-in God's pocket now, Ma'am. You are safe,' says Pash.

'No,' says Ma'am. 'Without Angus . . . what's the point?' she says and reaches for Pash's hand.

'Hush, Ma'am, it's okay,' says Pash.

'Watch Rosie, watch Rosie,' says Ma'am and she takes her last breath.

In all this horror, I imagine I can hear Maria's small voice. She never wanted anything like this. She wanted a simple life with Mansoor and Che Aminah, and now there is all this savagery, blood, and death. She would never have wanted anyone injured, all this destruction. All of this caused by wild, unresolved disagreements.

Chapter Twenty-Six

MEI MEI

1950

Singapore

After the riots, there are burned cars and smashed businesses and so many injured. The dead are being buried, honoured by different traditions. During the funeral service for Sir and Ma'am, Zandstra stands in the pew behind me with Anne. I am holding Rosie, she is looking at the people in the row behind. She is getting bigger and is squirming. She catches sight of Zandstra's tie, she reaches for it. It is long and pokes out of his blazer. She leans past me, looking up at Zandstra for some sort of recognition. She is trying to communicate with him. I turn to look behind me and Zandstra sneers. With his large hands, he holds Rosie's little wrist and starts to twist and twist. She tries to take her arm back, her face going from openness to distrust, then to pain. I know I have to get Rosie away, away from Zandstra.

Pash is supporting the Anglican priest as a server. I catch his eye as the priest asks everyone to rise. As the congregation stands lethargically to sing Ma'am's favourite hymn, 'Be Thou My Vision', our singing is drowned out by torrential rain. As I hold on to Rosie, pacing my breath in the humidity, I wonder if Ma'am ever truly loved Sir or Honour or even Rosie, and what made her want to be with the dreaded Zandstra.

After the service, the principal players of the expatriate and Asian business community stand in their mud-soaked shoes at the cemetery grounds. There is one last eulogy to put their souls to rest. Vee holds a sleeping Rosie and stands next to Aunt Faith. There is a heaviness in everyone's gaze as if the heat and despair have played tricks on our minds and rewired them to work in slow motion. I search for dry shelter under a saga seed tree. Its curved green pods are slowly turning brown, others have split, revealing the bright red seeds Honour and I collected: to us, the candy-coloured seeds were as precious as gold.

Despite the rain, pearls of perspiration form in the small of my back and seep, at first gently then in what feel like torrents, down the shallow trail of my spine and in between my buttocks. Arching away from the damp of my dress, I feel Pash's gaze. With my head bowed down I see thick, red mud stuck to his white robe.

I shift my weight back towards my heels and lock my lower jaw into place. I hold my elbows tightly across my chest. I know Honour will be leaving now for good. As the rain hammers down, I allow the sadness to fill my heart. I choke back fear, knowing I will be left behind. We need to act fast.

Back at the house, after the service and burial, I sit on my cot in front of my little mirror. It is a desperate situation. We have no masters. Sir, Ma'am, they are gone, my employers are dead. What happens to me? Zandstra is still a threat. How will I manage getting Rosie away from him? I look straight into the little mirror and am shocked to see Anne, Anne Zandstra, and Aunt Faith in the reflection.

'You deserve better,' says Anne.

'Mrs Zandstra Ma'am?' I ask.

'You, Rosie, all of us, deserve better, a better life,' says Aunt Faith. 'You were a brave girl, Mei Mei.'

'How do you mean?' I ask. 'I couldn't help Sir and Ma'am. What are you . . . what can I do?'

'Zandstra. He is a monster. There is no stopping him, he will come looking for Rosie,' says Anne. 'You need to get her away from this place, away from my husband. Take my advice, take my money, and get her out of here.'

Anne gives me more money than I've ever seen.

'Take it,' she says. 'And take Rosie.'

'I will,' I say and take this woman's money.

Aunt Faith nods in my direction then walks back out and along the walkway back to the main house tripping over a second shrine Cook has set up. I hear her talking to herself as she walks.

'I understand they have to keep out the damn evil spirits, but there's no need to burn the bloody incense all day and all night. What good does that do if the devil is already inside the house,' says Aunt Faith.

I couldn't agree more with this old woman.

Chapter Twenty-Seven

MEI MEI

1950

Singapore

Hurry, Mei Mei, I tell myself. It's time. Now's my chance. I pull Rosie's cotton dresses, her underclothes, and cloth diapers out from under my mattress. I've been holding them back from the laundry pile, waiting for the right moment. I've got to move fast and not forget anything.

Rosie's clothes are so light in my hands. I choose my favourite dress of hers to put on her, the one with the front smocking, with little prints of strawberries and white flowers on a bed of green leaves. The soft fabric smells like her, like vanilla and a hint frangipani, the white blossoms still warm from the day's sun. I roll her clothes tightly together and line the bottom of the Royal Basmati rice bag with more things she will need. A bar of soap and a small comb.

The bottom of the bag smells like rice and the earth, but there is a sourness to the smell that I don't like, but I don't have the time to find a different bag. This one works. It has long, thick handles that I can loop over my shoulders to keep my hands free for Rosie. I'll be responsible for the bag and for carrying

Rosie until we get to the border. Then Mr Today will take her, she'll sleep in the sarong, safe, in the arms of Mr Today, until I can make my way back to her after the three of us finish the other task.

I need her pacifier. She's always losing it, so if I can find a second one, I'd better put two in the bag. *Where did I last see it?* The blanket will be hard to pack. Maybe I'll just wrap her in it. It's made of a thicker cotton with a nubbed, waffle pattern. Rosie also has a favourite soft toy I need to bring. It's a little blue bunny with long ears she likes to suck on. Before I wake her, I'll add more cloth diapers to the rice bag.

I don't need much. My doll, only if there's room. Water. I have a flask for water. It's heavy, but I can wedge it in the side of the bag. I've got a pack of Marie biscuits. Rosie likes to chew on these. She rubs them against her gum line and makes them into a gooey paste, a real mess.

More food for Rosie. Formula, just enough for the crossing, then she'll need more. She has started to try mango, just a bit mashed up in her fist to suck on. I'll check the cooling room before we leave and take a couple more. I hope Rosie sleeps on the way over.

I lean over her crib to wake her, to gather her in my arms. Her drowsy eyes are still clouded by new waking. I struggle with the height of the railing on the crib and step on the footstool to lift her up. She's getting heavier every day, the weight of her body on my child hips comforts me. 'I will keep you safe,' I say as I carry her. I lift the rice bag over my shoulders and take the back staircase towards the rear of the property, to the garage and the waiting car. With the guilt money Ma'am has given me and the money from Anne Zandstra, I take this baby. I am going to keep her safe. Suleiman gets me across into Johor Bahru, and from there, I hand Rosie to Mr Today who has brought one of his girls. Together they bring Rosie on a bus to Ipoh.

'Goodbye, sweet Rosie,' I tell her. 'I'll be right back.'

It is dawn when I arrive back at the house from the border. I walk down to the pool deck to sweep and I am confronted with a sight I have never seen. The usual clear water reveals thousands and thousands of moths, their bodies and wings translucent from the chlorine are writhing on top of the pool. The temperature has changed ever so slightly and the winds have moved just enough to thrust these insects into taking a suicidal leap into the water. I stand by the side and scoop away the dead bodies. Some of the insects are still alive and writhe around towards a dry surface, catching themselves in the drains. It is revolting to see this flailing. I heap their chlorine-bleached bodies onto the edge of the pool. I can see the bottom now.

As I scoop the last of the dead insects, I see the dummy, Rosie's pacifier. It is yellow and blue. It rocks gently at the bottom of the swimming pool directly below me. It's as if Rosie leaned over to look at her reflection, opened her mouth, and released the dummy to the bottom of the deep end. The dummy lying there at the bottom of the pool gives me an unpleasant feeling, like I need to vomit, and I am suddenly very afraid of my own thinking.

'No!' I yell, 'No! No! Rosie! No!'

Ling Li walks then runs down towards the pool deck.

'Rosie! No!' I keep yelling.

Suleiman and Cook come running.

'The dummy, look!' I point at the bottom of the pool.

'It must have fallen from her mouth, where's Vee?' asks Ling Li.

Vee comes to the pool deck out of breath.

'Vee!' I scream my face getting red.

'Vee!' says Cook.

'What did you do, Vee? Vee, you were in charge of looking after Rosie, you!' Ling Li is wailing.

'What you mean, I never . . .' says Vee.

Zandstra is near the front gate and walks through the gardens to the pool towards the wailing.

'What is going on?' he asks.

'The baby, someone's taken her,' says Cook.

'She's been drowned,' screams Ling Li. 'Vee, Vee was supposed to be watching her.'

'Where is she, where is Rosie?' he demands. 'You, did . . . did you drown her?' Zandstra points to Vee.

'No,' says Vee. 'Never.'

'She's responsible, Sir,' says Ling Li. 'Vee, Sir. Vee is responsible,' she says. 'She is supposed to watch the baby.'

'I'm not responsible. I'd never do such a thing, you know that, Ling Li,' she says.

We watch as the two women who cared for baby Rosie tear into each other. Cook and Suleiman hold Ling Li and Vee apart. There is so much commotion and running around, looking for Rosie, calling her name out across the gardens and in every room. The police are called. To me, they look no different from the thugs who beat Sir and Ma'am. Just their outfits are different: see-through blue polyester, their belts too stiff, their boots track mud into the servants' quarters.

'Sir, the baby's dummy at the bottom of the pool, we found it, leading us to suspect this woman for taking the child,' said one of the officers pointing at Vee.

'Take this one away!' says Zandstra.

The police drag Vee by the armpits, her breasts flop across her chest, her upper lip is covered in sweat. Thunder rackets across the skies as Vee's screams and grunts reach all our ears. Everyone is crying and exhausted. By the end of the chaos, we sit with our heads in our hands and watch as the police drive off with Vee. There is just one more thing we need to do.

Chapter Twenty-Eight

ISABELLE GOH

1999

London

Yes, Detective, before you cast shame my way, I *was* complicit in the false accusation, we all were. I admit, I took advantage of Vee. She had never done anything to harm me. She had only shown me true kindness, and I had failed to protect her. We all had. Years later, at the cathedral, Pash and I agreed that after all the things, all the terrible things I have done in my life, it was this betrayal that weighed most on my conscience. He admitted to me the same failing, but it was a different time then, Detective, you have to understand that. It was an unforgiving time. What we did do was protect the most innocent of us all, Rosie.

I can't seem to feel my hands, Detective, or my feet. The numbness has turned now to nothing, nothing. The nurse, please if she is near, tell her to bring me more . . . more morphine, something for this pain of not feeling.

Now that Rosie is safe, and the household is distracted by the police taking Vee away, the three of us move on to the next necessary step, eradicating Zandstra. What we do would look like an accident. A bad fire. At least that's how we planned it.

The task over, Honour, Pash, and I race back from Malcolm Road to 24 Mount Rosie Road and hide in the palms near the swimming pool until the smoke subsides and Zandstra is found. We see Cook walk out from the house and down to the pool. He holds out Rosie's favourite biscuits and calls out her name into the trees, calling back her soul.

'Come, baby, I have your favourite treats with me. Your very favourite. Please come back, come to us, we want to hold you, please, baby Rosie, come, come back,' he calls out.

He then calls out Ma'am's name. 'Ma'am, I have your drink, the radio is on, come back, come back inside.'

Cook calls to the trees and into the jungle. 'Sir, time for your tea, come, the men are waiting in the study, come back, Sir,' he calls.

Tears stream down his face, his voice cracks. I choke back a silent sob. Cook is honouring the dead. What we have done deserves no praise. Zandstra can't hurt us any more, but Vee, Vee is now the blood on our hands. There is little investigation into the accident at the Zandstra residence. The police, the courts, everyone wants this tragedy to go away, no one has any energy for more sadness and death. 'The family has borne enough tragedy as it is,' people say.

All three of us went our separate ways: me to Malaya with Rosie, and Pash and Honour to the UK. There was no time for us to discuss what we had done, but that was for the best. Zandstra could no longer hurt anyone. I imagined Honour in her university room, staying up all night at a high desk with a lamp pulled down close to her papers. Knowledge would fill her head, letters would climb up and down pages in books and she would make sense of the human body and ways to heal. She had once told me that nursing could be in her future. I imagined her learning about medicines and how to care for sick people. And Pash in the UK with his cousin. Pash would keep studying with the church. But somehow, I thought Pash would give up religion and find his own path.

Chapter Twenty-Nine

MEI MEI

1951

Ipoh

It is dark when I get to Ipoh. The apartment where Mr Today keeps his girls is to be our new home, mine and Rosie's. My new role is to be a teacher. Not like Honour had been to me. Instead, I now teach hundreds of girls how to rinse, wash, remove stains, iron, fold, repeat. How to make beds, set a table. I am just another girl with a bit of experience. And Rosie, Rosie has so many mothers, so many little mothers to dote on her. They all want to hold her, to pinch her cheeks. When it is all too much, she reaches for me. My Rosie.

She has pale skin, and a blue-black spot on her back, just like mine. The maids call her 'little phoenix', referring to her eyes that turn up at the sides like the tail feather of the phoenix. I am indebted to Mr Today for keeping us under the radar. But I know that to keep Rosie I will have to lose myself. It's not forever, it's all we have for now.

'Too many eyes,' says Mr Today. 'Too many eyes and mouths know that you took the baby, Mei Mei.'

'Nobody knows, they won't care, too much bad blood, everyone will just wish it away, there has been too much tragedy already for the family,' I say.

'People don't forget so easily. You'll need a new identity. People will still come, looking for you,' he says.

'I'll change my name,' I say. 'A grown-up person's name, a real name.'

'Like what?' he asks, laughing.

I think of the names I know. Ling Li, Honour, Tessa, Maria, Faith, Vee, Anne, and the woman from the Jesus group, what was her name? I remember Ling Li told me once. Isabelle. Yes, there it is.

'I've decided for myself,' I say.

'And?' he asks.

'I'm to be Isabelle,' I tell him.

'Ah ha,' he nods. 'Isabelle . . . sounds good.'

'Goh,' I say. 'Goh like Ling Li's name.'

'What about Rosie, she'll need a new name,' he asks.

'Maria,' I say. 'Maria Roy.'

The new collection of girls sits back on their haunches, balancing their thin arms out over their knees, the way their fathers, mothers, uncles, and aunts all sit in their villages, their toes splayed out to balance their weight. They sit together. Rosie awakes in them a softness. They coo to her with shy smiles and giggles, remembering their own young family members. Mr Today calls them his supply, his product. They remind me of my former life, before I worked at the great house. Here in Ipoh, at the transfer station as Mr Today calls it, there is just enough food for the new recruits, and mats with clean sheets in the coolest part of the building for them to rest in between my lessons.

Mr Today costs out the detailed transaction fee for each girl. He keeps the paperwork in a satchel he wears across his chest like a badge of noble honour, but there's nothing noble about this operation. He keeps track of which girl has paid her full fee to Mr Today's Maid Service and, at his own whim, he can top up a girl's loan payment or dock future pay from her recruitment fee. It is an unfair system of checks and balances, of human transit, of human desperation, and I am playing a central role.

'Madame Isabelle!' says Mr Today.

'Ha! Come now,' I tell him.

'Well, that's your new name, isn't it?' he says.

'And?' I lift Rosie up on my hip.

'With your new identity, I need you to work now, I need you to find a way for my business to grow. People will be looking for the child, and . . .'

'And?' I ask.

'We need a plan to make money, more money so we can get her some schooling,' says Mr Today.

'She's not part of your business,' I tell him.

'Ha! You both are,' he says. 'I didn't stick my neck out to get nothing in return,' he says. 'Plus, Ling Li knows everything, she'll be wanting a cut.'

His smile falls away and I suddenly notice he looks older when he's not smiling. I have a sudden fear in my belly. *What have I done?* I think silently. Vee, innocent Vee, will be imprisoned and I've attached myself to a small-time crook. I wonder if I've simply traded Zandstra for a different kind of evil. I play it cool.

'We are branching out, Mei Mei. I want my own agency. And that's where you come in. I need a direct line to employers, Miss Isabelle. In Singapore. To European houses, the wealthy Chinese. So many families need household help,' he says. 'You know how it works.'

'I don't, I don't know,' I say.

'But that's where you came from,' he says.

'Yes, but I never knew, I never knew how it all works. All I knew was the Jesus lady brought us to the great house,' I tell him.

'Well, find out more,' he demands.

'Find out how to sell your girls?' I ask.

'They aren't for sale, for rent,' he corrects me.

'How does it work from your end?' I ask.

'I am the recruiter,' he says. 'I source the supply, feed, and train. Then agency pays me . . . if I become agent, I make more money, no more middleman.'

'Then you pay me to teach the girls?' I ask.

'Exactly, lah,' he tells me like it's the easiest thing in the world to understand. 'None of them have proper training. And they can practise taking care of Rosie.'

I realize then that I am both indispensable to him and that I am dependant on him, for now. In my life at the great house, I had access to people talking. They all talked about needing house help, and soon I am crossing the border from Malaya to Singapore often.

Mr Today fixes me up with fake documents. One blurry photo makes me a maid, another piece of identification and I am a recruiter, I am all things to all people. I meet with all manner of supply and demand and learn the business of supplying domestic workers. I learn that the girls come to Mr Today desperate. They hear from others that Singapore offers them a chance, a chance to make up to five to seven times more money than back home. What I learn is that Mr Today is paid a commission of almost a quarter of the girl's total earnings for two years, and that this fee is not paid upfront, but taken from the girl's monthly salary. It is an unfair burden, but for Mr Today, a lucrative business model.

I show the girls how to use an iron. I show them the scar on my arm to warn them with great effect. I show them how to use the laundry machine, how to remove all matter of stains with bleach, with salt, with vinegar, with soda, how to fold. The girls like the fact that I am a maid just like them and that I can show them how to make a master extra pleased.

Moving between Singapore and Malaya during those early years working for Mr Today, the business grows, and we move from being recruiters into starting an agency. I rent a small apartment in Geylang where rents are cheaper and I don't know anyone. I buy a used microwave and vacuum cleaner, and bring the girls from the agency back to sleep in the apartment. I keep a tight budget and the girls sleep like sardines on mats on the floors, sharing rice and eggs. When I have time, after Mr Today's Maid Agency is closed, I teach them to cook.

It is crowded in the apartment at night and I need a place to myself. After I lock the girls in for the night, I walk to the closest hawker centre. At my favourite booth, a quiet Chinese woman with a sweet smile serves me. We rarely speak, but I see her at the food court every night.

One particular night, there is an altercation at one of the tables. A group of men are getting drunk on cheap tins of beer and start to pick a fight. One of them over turns a red plastic table and it bounces on the cement floor and a fistfight begins. The next thing I know another man holds up a machete and starts hacking one of the other men. There is so much blood. I sit frozen to the spot. I am afraid of drawing any attention to myself and I pretend none of the violence has occurred. I know better than to get involved.

The man lies on his side bleeding out. Deep brown blood seeps across the floor. The attacker and the other men race away leaving the machete behind. Then I watch as the Chinese woman at the booth walks calmly towards the severely injured man and burns his face with the stub of her cigarette, five times. This woman, this small unassuming woman has been so cruel and yet so calm. I channel this way of being and it sticks. There is only hardship ahead. I have sold out to a hardened heart. My imagination has shut down.

These years are hard and as much as I try to fight it, my heart is turning brittle like the inside of a cracked walnut, the chambers crumbling at the slightest pressure. I look at myself in the bathroom mirror one day and see that my own lips make the same shape that Ma'am's lips had made, mocking me one too many times. My lips are the same curled lips from the woman from the hawker stall when she burned the man at the food court in Geylang.

Chapter Thirty

MEI MEI

1951

Singapore

To build my own business, separate from Mr Today, I need to be successful and I need to be ruthless. Competitors soon get wind of the money to be made, so I need to be creative to stay ahead of the pack. There is the usual way by making up reasons to dock pay, or increase the endless series of fees needed to get a girl placed. I am a part of this system of degradation, parading the girls in the maid agency window forcing them to mimic simple household tasks, like puppies performing in the pet shop window.

I know the girls are too afraid to speak up. I was once one of these girls. I also know that other agencies treat their supply far worse and get ahead financially, so I need a way to advertise, somewhere discreet, to legitimize my new operation, and make more money. The girls talk about the mission services at the churches when they get to Singapore and I learn that St Andrew's is fast becoming one of the churches that supports domestic workers. It is also the church for the rich families.

I get close to the missionaries. I know their affinity for tea and pay visits, ingratiating myself into their circles. I am soon able to advertise my services in the church newsletter. My calling card is that I supply Christian maids. Other churches allow me to advertise, assuming I am a Christian maid agency. I follow the assumptions and that becomes my niche.

Within eight short months, all my girls have been placed, all the paperwork and the costs are checked and balanced. One girl, Stella, stays behind in Ipoh and becomes my helper with Rosie. She is slow, but kind and devoted to Rosie's needs. I am free to develop and push my own business forward. There is an endless supply of our product. The girls I place ask me to help their sisters and friends, cousins, and soon my own agency, Goh Goh Maids, becomes a direct competitor to Mr Today's Maid Service. I move to a larger apartment with more room for more girls. I hire a Mandarin tutor to teach Rosie. Soon Goh Goh Maids becomes the preferred service provider in Singapore. I am getting more and more work and I am a success.

As the years pass by, I have enough money to buy an industrial building in Bedok and a small property where Master Tong used to live. The government in Singapore grants me citizenship, the business with Rosie long forgotten. I move into the new building with our living quarters on a second level apartment and the girls and the training facility at the bottom. Rosie is at day school and life is good.

One day, I come back to my apartment carrying clothing I had made for the trainees of Goh Goh Maids. Lavender uniforms, with purple aprons. Mr Today is waiting for me. I walk straight past him and towards my room.

'Where do you think you're going?' says Mr Today.

'And good to see you too,' I say.

'You're messing with my operation, this isn't the way it works,' he says.

'Oh, and what way is that?' I ask.

'That you work for me,' he stabs his forefinger in my face.

I walk towards my locked bedroom.

'Where are you going?' he asks.

'To my room?' I say.

'Don't walk away from me!' he shouts.

He comes up behind me, and pins me against the locked door. He is muscular and easily able to overpower me. I have the key in my hand, but as I am carrying large packages, I am stuck. I have to drop the bags to open the door and I am tired. I know what he wants and so I let him in. I give in. I don't put up a fight, in fact, I make him want me more. I tell him to sit in the chair next to my double bed.

I lock the door and straddle the bed, my back towards him, I take off my underclothes leaving my clammy T-shirt on. I turn my back to him and twirl my hips around and around, showing him glimpses of my young, strong body. I succumb to his power, but in this act of surrender I learn from him more of the maid trade inside and out. I learn who and how to bribe, how to stay above the law while extorting where needed and how to make even more money to keep Rosie safe.

As I transform from Mei Mei into Isabelle, I build up my coffers. I pay myself for all the secrets I have had to keep that have rotted inside me. I use multiple bank accounts in the names of the maids. I have their names, identities. I collect people. I hold their futures in my hands, I control their lives. I learn how to use others to my advantage. I am a chameleon. The missionaries open their trusting hearts to me. The girls see me as one of them and share their hardships, their hopes and aspirations for a bright future. The recruiters and agents and I achieve a mutual respect and the regulators see me as a hard-working businesswoman. I am a success on all sides. As a result of this work, I have the first official, government-sanctioned maid agency. I supply foreign workers to clean all the government buildings. An amazing turn of events—this keeps me ahead of the growing competition of maid agencies.

As Rosie grows, it is harder to hide her in plain sight. She is a beautiful creature. Her nickname sticks and she is known affectionately as little phoenix. Her black hair, fair skin, and strong bones are combined with light coloured eyes, like mine. I need to get her a proper education. I see an opportunity to reach out through the church connection to find Pash and take a big chance.

One of the women from the mission service helps me write to the church office in Singapore with a request for Pash's address in London. And within a few months, I receive my first letter from him. Our correspondence is always very formal. I enquire whether he has the ability to support the education of a young Malaysian girl named Maria Roy and sign it Goh Enterprises Ltd.

Pash doesn't disappoint. Through his connections with the church, a boarding school in the UK grants her tuition and accommodation and doesn't ask too many questions. I register Maria Roy with a new birth date and build a profile as her guardian. Then I step away. My work is done, she is on her way. Now it's over to Pash. He had always said from the get-go that he would help. It is hard to let her go, but I do. I wait for the annual letter from Pash to Goh Enterprises Ltd with the update on our co-contribution to the future of Maria Roy.

Part IV

MURDER

Chapter Thirty-One

ISABELLE GOH

1970

Singapore

The façade of the mall is blackened by months of rain. The automatic glass doors are broken. Inside, the mall is dark with mildewed concrete. The main set of stairs has been replaced with a rickety set of escalators and there are no windows to the outside. I walk behind a group of Malay matrons dragging their feet across the tile floor, wearing the weight of the world under their snug headscarves.

Maid agencies run along every corridor for five stories. Young women sit at each window, their young faces looking eager and anxious at once, but mostly dejected. They wear the uniform of different agencies, yellow cotton shirts at Expat Maids, white tops with pink borders over at Raymond Maids.

Red and yellow decals spell out GOH GOH MAIDS on the original sign up ahead. It is my first agency and where I keep my office.

At the front of the space, I have created a seating area with cheap plastic vinyl cushions. The new girls sit in a row. Some look downcast, others hopeful, others plain scared, hoping someone will choose them, pick them, and with one decision change the direction of their lives forever.

I enter the office and head to my desk cluttered with papers and files. The garish lighting overhead and the glass tabletop make everything feel temporary and precarious. I feel as if my fist could come down on the tabletop and shatter the dreams of all these young girls.

A hopeful maid sits in the window closest to the door. She has fuzzy black hair cropped at her cheekbones. Her broad face and wide-set eyes indicate that she must be from the tribal hill tracts of the northern border, somewhere between Myanmar and Bangladesh. I am sitting at my desk when a well-dressed, older Caucasian woman enters the waiting area. The young maids sit up straighter and put on their kindest faces.

My face is painted too. I have taken to sporting a black wig, although I think it looks natural. It is voluminous, giving me height, and the make-up I wear every day to cover my scar tissue and the mark on my face has become part of my armour. My false eyelashes touch the insides of my overly large, slightly tinted glasses. My lips are painted a coral pink.

'Hello, Madame, please have a seat. How may I address you?' I ask the woman.

The woman sits down across from me. She holds a brown leather purse, both hands securing her handbag snug against her thighs.

'You can call me Anne,' she answers.

'We have new girls, best option. You train as you like,' I say. 'Your husband's employer has recommended my agency?'

She looks familiar to me, but I can't place her, not yet.

'That's right,' the woman says, although I don't believe her.

'Thank you for the recommendation. Please take a look at our catalogue,' I say.

I slide a bright pink binder across my desk. The woman looks haphazardly through the pages of photographs and biodata of girls not looking for what she really needs when I hear her whisper my name.

'Mei Mei,' she says quietly.

'We have new supply of maids, you see, they are good workers, hard workers.'

'It's me,' says the woman.

I am terrified someone has found out my ruse, that everything has caught up to me, but who is this woman?

'It's the heat, the cockroaches, keeping your home clean and the food shopping, everything much harder in the heat,' I tell her.

'Much harder,' she nods.

I look closely and see it is Anne. Anne Zandstra. After all these years, she still has the same short haircut and simple jewellery. I get up and walk past the maid at the storefront and lock the door of the agency. My heart sinks.

'Mei Mei,' she sighs. 'It has been so many years, how . . .'

'Yes. How did you find me?' I ask her.

I return to my desk and sit across from Anne.

'Oh, you're easy to find,' she says laughing. 'But, it's not you I'm looking for,' she says coughing into a worn tissue.

The memory of Zandstra screaming hits me, the smoke billowing out of a bathroom window. I feel trapped now, like I need her to leave for me to compartmentalize that memory like it never happened.

'You, you children did the impossible, you took down the weight around my neck. Zandstra died, later that day, you know. He was in agony. You three, you are responsible for a murder and a disappearance and now I . . . I want to know, how did my investment turn out?' says Anne.

I panic. It has been two decades and I am still terrified of his name, Zandstra. We did our best to end him, we were so young and he was so much stronger.

'Your investment?' I ask.

'Yes, the money I paid to ensure Rosie's safety and yours,' says Anne. 'You remember, don't you?'

'Your guess is as good as mine. I don't know where she is, I have let her go, better that way,' I say to Anne.

'I understand that,' she says. 'But surely you know where she is.'

'No, we, I don't know where she is,' I say. 'I'm not sorry, he was . . .'

'He was cruel and a monster, but you children were equally cruel,' says Anne.

'We were just children . . . Excuse me, will there be anything else?' I get up and head to the door.

'The wrong person was accused, Mei Mei, you are not innocent,' says Anne.

Anne glares at me, she is right, none of us are innocent, just slightly angry most of the time.

'You helped me get Rosie to safety,' I say.

'Which is why I am here to find out how my investment paid off. There are few things in life I am curious about and she is one of them,' says Anne. 'And if you don't tell me, I *will* go to the police.'

'No one cares any more. There are far worse things happening in the world now, Anne,' I say. 'Thank you for your concern.'

'You underestimate people's appetite for a good ending, Mei Mei. Don't think people have forgotten, the past is never forgotten,' says Anne.

I have been found out. A sign perhaps. Time for me to extract myself from this place. Time to move on. Anne might be a threat, but I need to reach for a bigger challenge. I want more.

For years I have suppressed my imagination. I have put my head down, worked hard, learned the business of moving girls and women across borders without detection or at least no detection of serious wrongdoing. I have learned how to loan money, to put pressure on weak links to make a substantial return. My life is set up the way I have always wanted. I have purple sheets with matching curtains and my own helpers. Rosie is grown and I can breathe without looking over my shoulder. So when Anne shows up, I am surprised to see flickers of my old imagination come alive again, but they are all the images I wish to forget. Boiled tripe, unborn chicks, the smell of Zandstra, and the sound of a broken wing against a cardboard box. I feel trapped.

The same day Anne Zandstra comes to my maid agency, Ling Li shows up at my apartment. It's been years since I've seen Ling Li. Her hair has gone white and her eyes are bloodshot.

'Mr Today looking for you, ah,' says Ling Li.

'I'd be worried if he wasn't,' I say.

'You compete with him, now he's mad,' says Ling Li.

'I'm on my own now, my own business,' I say.

'On your own?' Ling Li laughs. 'No one on their own. You make more money, more money now than Mr Today? You buy land?' she asks.

'I have a building, yes,' I tell her.

'How much?' she asks,

'Ling Li, my business now, ah,' I say.

'Mei Mei, how much,' she asks.

'It's Isabelle,' I say.

'What?' she asks.

'My name,' I say.

'Isabelle?' she says. 'Where is Rosie?'

'I don't know,' I tell her.

For years I have just received an annual update from Pash. Rosie is doing fine. That's all I need to hear.

'I care for her, too, where is she?' asks Ling Li.

'I honestly don't know,' I reply.

'You don't know? You don't know? What you mean? I saved you, I cared for you, you cared for Rosie, so where is she?' Ling Li demands.

'I cannot say,' I tell her.

I stay silent as she fumes. She stands up and overturns papers and documents on my desk, sending glassware to the floor, smashing what she can until she stops and falls back onto the chair.

'Mr Today sent me,' she says. 'He wants to break you.'

I am afraid now.

'Why? Why can't everyone just leave me, leave me alone?' I ask.

'You're the winning ticket,' she says. 'Now, everyone is interested. The only way to keep him from ruining you is to join him. I told him you would be open to it,' says Ling Li.

'You don't own me, no one does,' I tell Ling Li.

Ling Li sits down heavily on the chair beside my bed.

'What do you take me for? You think I was never tempted to break out on my own?' says Ling Li.

'What?' I ask.

'Of course I was. When I met Mr Today, he ask me to join. The tattoo, the butterfly on my shoulder, my gold chain? I am owned, too, you are owned. None of us are free,' says Ling Li.

'I am my own person now,' I say calmly.

'You think that, but it's not true. We are all just links in a chain that the big guys tighten around our necks, and they will. You Mei Mei, you are a threat to them now. I'm here to warn you, you're just part of their web, and you can't get out,' says Ling Li.

'What is it really, Ling Li?' I ask.

'You have no choice,' says Ling Li. 'You must join Mr Today.'

'Ling Li, no!' I tell her.

'Yes, or I go to police and tell them you kidnapped Rosie, and that you kids . . .' says Ling Li.

'We did it for her own safety, you know what Zandstra was like,' I tell her.

'You, go back into business with Mr Today and his patrons, understand?' says Ling Li.

I had no choice, Detective. Anne Zandstra had me cornered. Ling Li had warned me that I had to partner again with Mr Today and, soon after, things went sideways fast. I moved too quickly, became too greedy much too soon. When one of Mr Today's business partners came to invite me to meet with one of the Quek brothers, a senior player at the next level of business partnerships, I was open to new possibilities.

His name was Robson Quek, not to be confused with his brother, Martin. I could tell the minute I first met Robson that I was in trouble. He had the same dangerous scent about him as Zandstra, the smell that made me acutely aware of my own safety. I felt small and fragile like a mouse deer being cornered by a much larger animal. Robson was a big-time gangster, not a petty crook. His family had land in Hong Kong and he wanted to find a way to turn a quick profit, to manipulate the system in his favour, and that meant a nimble partner who could find their way through the levels of bribery and coercion without notice and delay. I agree to meet Robson in his office in the Tanglin Shopping Centre.

I show up at the address I was given and enter a world that I had never been exposed to. The storefront is covered from floor to ceiling with framed artwork. There are sculptures on the floor and antique furniture. Maps and other fine art prints cover the tall countertops.

'Isabelle?' he says, reaching for both my hands.

'Good, good to meet you,' I say. His hands feel cold and boney.

'I understand you may want to grow your business to Hong Kong?' he asks.

'I have some early plans, yes,' I lie.

'Well, I am open to a conversation,' he says.

'I'm open to listen,' I say.

Robson is charming. Over lunch, he tells me about his brother and his plans to develop his business interests in Hong Kong and eventually in Europe.

'We have land that needs developing on the Kowloon side and we need a partner. You have capital you can invest with us and I can promise you great returns,' he says.

'Why me, why would you want to go into business with me? I'm nobody,' I say.

'Precisely. You are not known, you have no baggage, plus you have excellent potential. I've watched you manage risk for what looks like great reward,' says Robson.

'Yes,' I say.

He is convincing, saying all the right things. I feel very unsophisticated. Where he is at ease in the plush chairs and carpeted hotel restaurant, I am awkward and unglamorous. 'What do you say, Isabelle, ready to hear more?' he asks.

Chapter Thirty-Two

ISABELLE GOH

1999

London

Of course, I wanted more, Detective, of course, I did. I wanted all of it. I was moving on, moving on to real money, real power. Out of the small stakes of the Straits with Mr Today and out into the big time, Hong Kong, China, the world. Away from unreadable threats from Anne and Ling Li and forward. I could curate a whole new Isabelle. Worldly and ruthless. I knew linking up with the Quek brothers was dangerous, but I had overcome danger before and needed a new challenge.

'I'm in,' I said before thinking about how I would ever get out.

From what I first understand, this new business environment is just a different game, keeping score with a new playbook. I tabulate what is owed. I take chances on who to lean on, what I can gain. It is just a novel way to map out allegiances. What is different is that I soon learn that I owe my life to the company, to the Queks, and that my 'clients' owe me theirs. It is similar to how I operated the maid agencies, just with higher stakes and I am at the lowest rung of this new operation.

When the Queks' clients don't pay me back, I activate the next level of the game. The game is based on fear and it turns out I am very good at it. I start with threats, then violence, extortion, and kidnapping. People don't expect my pixie face and sideways smile to come knocking. I am the one who calls in the thugs while calmly filtering through peoples' belongings, taking what I want. Cries and pleas just bounce right off me. My world grows darker and my new currency is violence.

The first time I had to prove myself to the Queks and their boss, Mr Neo, I had to dance. It was a sure way for them to humiliate me. Somehow, I was able to block out the vileness around me. 'It's just another game,' I told myself. I played the game as a way of moving towards more power and glory and riches, more for Rosie. I pulsated and shifted and quivered like nobody's business. Whatever I was doing seemed to impress Mr Neo. He asked me to take care of some business in Hong Kong.

Hong Kong was brighter and taller than Singapore. Industry of every kind was in the air. People hustled for everything. The hotel in Wan Chai had scarlet-coloured wallpaper, this I would never forget. I was being tested. My test was to wait in the lobby for three days for instructions. Making me wait was a way of controlling my loyalty. I couldn't leave the hotel. Staff brought me food and accompanied me to the restroom. I was denied any rest and I passed the test. New tests continued.

In Mr Neo's world, luxury was the new language. I was about to enter the world of excess. I saw riches I never thought existed. Cars, art work, yachts, luxury handbags, watches, these were symbols I needed to learn; not just what they were but what they represented. I was a quick student. I also needed to learn to discern a fake from an original. And from here, I continued my training by entering a closeted society of businessmen trafficking humans, drugs, weapons. This was the big time and it both terrified and excited me. The vocabulary and rules of the game just kept shifting and I learned as I went. There were deals to be made and Mr Neo had determined I was of value. Unobtrusive and not someone you would ever expect to aid and abet such ruthlessness.

Business with Mr Neo and the Quek brothers meant that my investments were now inextricably linked with theirs. It also meant that I was always watched. I was given a bodyguard. You've met him, Detective, Charlie, Charlie Xiao. I had no immediate knowledge of where my money was going until months later, when I realized we were now an underground lending agency, a loan service for those who couldn't borrow from any established bank.

My initial work with the maid agencies was moving people across borders. It came with threatening families until they paid their fair share for their daughter's bond, but this bank, this business was much more nefarious. The distance between me and my money and the loan became further and further out of my reach.

I began my exit strategy five years into the agreement with the brothers, but it turns out that when you are in bed with devils, they never let you leave, they wrap their arms around your waist and entice you back with warm assurances of how much you are needed, they stroke you and cradle you in their arms and tell you that you are the most desired woman on earth and then hell really starts.

Even though I was travelling and involved in a world of distorted evil, I still received my annual update from Pash on Rosie's progress. That had been our agreement. Once she was at school, he would continue as her guardian, supporting her. In one of my cryptic responses, I told him I needed a way out from the uptight voices and locked throats, to get off the grid. I needed to

stay out of the devil's orbit or so I thought. I realized I didn't want
to turn into one of Queks' fallen angels.

Charlie and I knew too much about the underground bank
and their clients in the arms trade. It was all too much. Soon we
were warned that we had been added to the Quek brothers' kill
list. Many of the co-investors with the Queks were also looking
to get out and looked to invest in real estate in London as an
exit strategy.

Here is where we are connected again, Detective. It was
your Dom who stepped in. Dom's world overlapped with
mine along the fringes. He helped me find my St James's Place
apartment. How is he by the way? Please send him my regards.
Oh, I feel . . . the light, the light coming in pierces the back
of my eyes. My vision is cloudy. Could you please keep those
curtains shut?

The St James's flat was private, I could come and go from the
underground parking. The fact that my neighbours were royalty or
landed gentry meant that I created a buffer around me. Much more
interesting personalities surrounded me and that meant I could go
back and forth unnoticed. The other perfect undercover element
was Charlie's son. Little Tom needed an education and I offered to
help. I am not ashamed that I borrowed my bodyguard Charlie's
son as a ruse for me to be a benevolent matriarch. My new identity
was set. Tom became my make-believe grandson, little Tom.

Tom was a perfect reason to stay put in the UK. He needed
an education. It had worked the first time with me reaching out
to Pash and so I risked it again and asked Pash for help. Pash
delivered. This time I could pay full price and Tom got a spot as
a day pupil at the most prestigious day school in London. Your
Zoe is a year or two ahead of Tom, isn't she? I could play the role
of devoted grandmother. But to someone like me who was used
to looking over my shoulder my whole life, I missed the edge,
pushing against the margins, looking for pain, for profit. It was
too easy. One meeting with the headmaster of the top school

and I was in. Into a new circle, a new game. The headmaster had spent time in Malaysia as a child. I soon had him eating out of the palm of my hand, with the promise of a sizable donation. It was obscene.

Here was my new underground pet project while this boy, Tom, this 'grandchild' had a good enough education. New money from mainland China was rushing in on all sides, you should know, Detective, as your husband was involved in it too. Don't think I don't know. But my success in London was being thwarted. I was being blamed by the Queks for every failing their businesses experienced. Now I was the hunted. The Queks' took ruthless action. The industrial warehouses I had in Singapore were left to rot, no one would take up a maintenance contract. My world and finances were becoming smaller and there was nothing I could do except stay hidden.

/ # Chapter Thirty-Three

DETECTIVE AYESHA NUR

1999

London

When Interpol calls, Ayesha is away for the weekend, up in the Lakes District with her parents and Zoe. A long-awaited holiday for everyone. Ayesha needs a break. She takes a phone call from the gas station where she is filling up her car.

'Detective Nur?' says a man's voice with a French accent.

'This is she,' she says.

'Christian Gaul,' says the voice.

'Christian, Christian who?' asks Ayesha.

'Interpol's Asia Chief,' he says.

She releases the trigger on the gas nozzle. She is shaken out of holiday mode and immediately back to work.

'Uh, yes,' she says.

'You are aware we are following the Goh case, Isabelle Goh?' he asks.

Ayesha can see Zoe pressing her little face up against the rear window, making faces. Ayesha sticks out her own tongue, one last show of defiance against—against what? She's not sure.

'I know now,' she replies.

'*Très bien*. I'll be summoning a group to meet you in Singapore. This bank has got wind that we are on top of them,' he says.

'I'm sorry where? Singapore? And which bank?' asks Ayesha.

'The Quek operation in Asia, in Singapore,' he says.

'Come again?' she asks.

'Isabelle Goh, she was involved in a much larger operation. They know they are being watched and are slowly folding up. We need to get ahead of all this. We'll need eyes, trained eyes on the ground,' he says.

'Understood,' she replies.

Ayesha can't believe what she is hearing. Her heart is really pumping, her whole body feels alive. 'An international case,' she says slowly. 'Interpol wants me on an international case.'

'Understood? Fantastic. You good to go to Singapore? You'll be notified of next steps on Monday. Have a pleasant weekend,' he says.

Ayesha stands there in the cold, looking at her family inside the car. With one phone call, everything has changed. She is in the thick of it now, what she always wanted, to be involved in a big case, hunting down the bad guys over a problem greater than herself. She wonders how she is expected to get back into the car like nothing has happened and carry on like it is a normal day, travelling on holiday with her parents and Zoe. She'll have to tell her parents to be watchful. Ayesha's phone buzzes. A text from Christian Gaul: `Keep your parents and daughter out of London.`

'Darling, let us pay for the gas,' says her father.

'No need, Dad, it's fine,' says Ayesha.

'Who was that on the phone?' asks her mother.

'Just work, a regular check in,' replies Ayesha.

'I thought you said no calls this weekend,' says her mother.

'No calls!' shouts Zoe from the backseat.

'It's all right, no more,' she says.

Most of Ayesha's work before this case was average detective work: rooting out loan sharks, idiots getting drunk and killing people, the odd kidnapping and gang assassination. She likened it to working in the human zoo. *What about this particular murder investigation warrants Interpol's involvement?* she wondered. *It doesn't make sense. Was Isabelle really leading such a dangerous operation? Perhaps Christian what's his face has mistaken me for someone else, except he was very specific about my parents and Zoe.*

After Ayesha settles Zoe into the bedroom, she sits in the shared sitting room in the bed and breakfast where her parents are making tea.

'Mum, Dad . . .' says Ayesha.

'Yes, darling, this is so wonderful, to get away, thank you,' says her mother.

'Yes, well . . . this time away, I will need you to stay on holiday a bit longer,' she says.

'What?' asks her father.

'With Zoe,' she says.

'How do you mean, Ayesha? What now?' asks her father.

'Dad, Mum, the investigation I'm leading, it's turning into something big, I'll need to head to London on Monday and on to Singapore,' she says.

'Oh, Ayesha,' says her mother.

'Singapore?' asks her father.

'Yes, and I know, I'll need to cut the holiday short and disappoint Zoe, believe me it's not what I would have wanted to happen. Please. Can you stay and look after Zoe, just for another week or so?' she asks.

'Of course, but now I'm worried. What are you getting yourself into, darling?' says her mother.

'It's a lot, and I'm right in the thick of it. Thank you, Mum, Dad . . .' she says.

'Of course, but please keep safe,' says her father.

Ayesha moves to close the door to the bedroom she is sharing with Zoe.

'I said lights out Zoe, good night,' Ayesha says.

'Come sit with me for a minute,' says Ayesha's father. 'Zoe will be fine.'

'Thank you, it means the world to me,' says Ayesha.

Chapter Thirty-Four

DETECTIVE AYESHA NUR

1999

Singapore

Ayesha has never travelled to Asia before. She is immediately impressed by the level of order, the new infrastructure, and modernity of Singapore. She meets Detective Jimmy Ibrahim when she lands. He has a familiar way about him, open, self-deprecating. Not what she expected.

'That's some heat you've got here,' says Ayesha.

'Funny, today is cool, just 28 degrees Celsius,' says Jimmy.

'My core body temperature has just risen by twenty degrees,' says Ayesha. 'So, when do we meet the team?' she asks.

'Team?' Jimmy laughs. 'You're looking at it. You and me. We are it.'

'You can't be serious,' she says.

'Sadly, yes,' he says. 'The state of international policing is a financial disaster, and there is very little any of us can do about money laundering, loan sharking, and now this underground banking industry, it's just a way of business. They just sent you here so they can tell their higher ups they're doing something about it. It's a losing battle I'm afraid.'

'What are we going to be able to do, just the two of us? I mean, Goh operated in grey capital, an underground bank, that's above my pay grade,' says Ayesha.

Ayesha feels like someone has kicked her in the chest. She has come all this way to fail. She's way out of her comfort zone. They won't be able to do what she had thought, but she responds to Jimmy. They hit it off straight away. She likes learning about his roots in Kampong Glam and his busy family life.

'You had lunch yet?' asks Jimmy.

'I could definitely eat, yes,' says Ayesha.

They head to the Changi Village hawker centre and enjoy a messy lunch of nasi lemak. She learns of his family, his love of Singapore, how the gangsters and money lenders are keeping him busy.

'What do you know of the case so far?' asks Jimmy.

'Let's see, I know that we have the victim of an attempted murder under twenty-four-hour watch in a hospital in central London, we know she is wanted by Interpol, which you tell me now is just us, you and me, and I know that this is not only a story of kidnapping, but also a much larger network of human trafficking and an underground banking industry that we can't do anything about,' says Ayesha.

'Simple, really,' says Jimmy, laughing.

'It's more than I can handle on my own,' says Ayesha.

'Don't forget Operation Goh, the Quek brothers and their stronghold, the drugs and illegal weapons trade,' says Jimmy.

'We are completely screwed, I mean we are both in over our heads,' says Ayesha.

'What else do you know, what is the true motivation behind all of this?' asks Jimmy.

'Isabelle Goh is a successful criminal mastermind,' says Ayesha.

'Really? Or is she just a survivor, trying to outrun her past?' says Jimmy.

'Oooh, I like how you are thinking, bringing it back to the true motivations behind Isabelle's actions,' says Ayesha.

'Let's start with what we know and build the story to get to the heart of it, the motivations of these guys, that's our only chance. We're on our own and we'll be fine,' says Jimmy.

'I'll take your lead. I don't have much to go on. But, when you lay it out like that . . . Isabelle, each time I spoke with her, she asked me about a person every time,' says Ayesha.

'Does this person have a name?' asks Jimmy.

'Rosie, a girl called Rosie,' says Ayesha.

'Rosie, Rosie, where could you be?' asks Jimmy.

'She'll be a grown woman now and may also go by a different name,' says Ayesha.

'I say we start there, with the reason behind Isabelle's compulsive striving,' says Jimmy.

'I've got some evidence, the photos,' says Ayesha.

'Your reports are very clear,' says Jimmy. 'That time in Singapore's history was around the Maria Hertogh riots.'

'Yes, Mei Mei, err . . . Isabelle told me about the time she met Maria, what a complicated time,' says Ayesha.

'All mostly forgotten now, no one wants to recollect bad memories. Maria is still alive and has had a very hard life,' says Jimmy.

'You've read my report, seen the old photos of the house at 24 Mount Rosie Road. Is that a place we can visit?' Ayesha asks.

'This grand estate, where Isabelle Goh worked as a girl, it's unreal. I mean you can't make this stuff up, it's like some sort of fairy tale—a rags to riches and back to rags story,' says Jimmy. 'We *can* go, but to get the full impression, we go on foot. Not in the heat of the day, but dusk, before the call to prayer,' says Jimmy.

They drive together and park on Chancery Lane next to a construction site. Ayesha sees men resting in the shade right on the sidewalk in front of her, the armies of itinerant workers building the future of Singapore. They walk up a winding road and Ayesha can sense history and the jungle rubbing up against each other. They pass a number of black-and-white estates. It is another world after the rush of the city. The great houses peek out through the dense fauna, hiding their history. Ayesha read that many of these stately homes were residences of the British colonial masters. Then, during the war, the Japanese army used some of these mansions as places to imprison comfort women to pleasure the troops. Ayesha shakes off the horror of this past.

'That house used to belong to a prominent Armenian family,' says Jimmy.

He is pointing to an enormous house on a vast piece of open land.

'I heard they left it to the church. Doubtful they'll sell, but the developers are circling like vultures. Big bucks to develop this land. Up here are some of the last of these huge estates. Ah, and here we are,' says Jimmy.

Something shifts in Ayesha, a form of awareness, a knowledge of this place. It is as if Ayesha has been here before, in a dream or in a former life. She knows this place, this landscape, the curvature of the road, the lives of the people who made this their home. Through heavy, wrought-iron gates Ayesha sees the expansive grounds. It is exactly how Isabelle described it to Ayesha. She can imagine Mei Mei running through the gardens with Dr H, when she was Honour, and Pash, before he was Bishop. Ayesha stops and slowly takes a breath. 24 Mount Rosie Road, she can't believe she is standing here. The magnificent house is surrounded by jungle, the mosque minaret behind it peeks over the tops of the vast trees.

Ayesha looks closer at the architecture, the placement of the building in and amongst the rise of the hill. She sees that the gardens seem to have recently been hacked back with no thought to any aesthetic. The paint and shutters are ill-kept. She thinks she sees an elliptical bike discarded under the raised area of the veranda.

'Impressive, isn't it?' asks Jimmy.

'I'm lost for words, it is truly amazing, it's exactly like she told me, like Isabelle told me,' says Ayesha.

'You know my mother worked in one of these grand houses, but they are all falling apart. No one wants to live in them any more. The government owns them all, but competing land resources . . . you get the picture,' says Jimmy. 'I will leave you to wander around. It is vacant, so you can go in. I'll find you later. Need to connect with a friend at the mosque. Be back soon.'

Ayesha stands at the front gate and takes in the winding driveway. She looks down the lane towards where the Zandstras' must have lived, up on Malcolm Road. Ayesha can feel Mei Mei, she can sense her presence. *How is this possible?* Ayesha asks herself. She hears a single bird calling, the koel. Underfoot, she feels broken egg shells.

Fire-red stalks of ginger plants and white frangipani trees line the driveway. Perfect white buds litter the pathway. Ayesha takes it all in. She feels dizzy and unsteady, she wonders how many hours she has been awake. She rights herself and walks up the drive towards the main house, standing under the veranda by the front doors to absorb it all.

Ayesha presses against the front doors and they open. She walks through the front foyer and sees curtains at the back of the house billow in and out with the rising breeze. She walks towards the back of the house across the red terracotta tiles then outside to the covered walkway to the kitchen house and the servants' quarters. Fans whir above her, but the heat is close. At the back of the house, the rooms are smaller. In one room, she sees a made-up mattress and simple belongings. Someone is here.

She returns to the main house along the covered walkway and up the backstairs to the second floor. The rise of each step is not easy even for Ayesha. She is a little out of breath when she reaches the upper floor and makes her way to the open veranda where shutters on the windows are half closed. She pushes them open to reveal a gorgeous vista of gardens, more beautiful trees and flowers and the view of a swimming pool. Ayesha imagines Mei Mei having to clean each window pane, one hundred and forty-four in all. From where she is standing, Ayesha sees a figure downstairs, near the swimming pool. She wonders who she is and if she has any recollection of the house and its inhabitants in years past.

Ayesha makes her way across the cool tiles over to the bedrooms. At the very tops of each bedroom wall, open tile fixtures let the breeze through. There are three large, empty bedrooms. Ayesha feels like she has been in each room before. She turns back to the open veranda and heads down the main staircase, stroking the elaborate woodwork on the banister and stands in the foyer facing the front doors. To her right is the living room, to her left is the dining room, and through the dining room is the study, with its bay windows and door that exits straight out onto a walled stone garden. Ayesha sits on the steps of the kitchen house and again feels like she knows this place. Jimmy finds her there as the sun shifts from glow to shadow.

'How do I know this place?' Ayesha asks him.

'I know what you mean. There is something about it that brings our senses alive,' he says. 'Must be our training kicking in. The craft of imagining others' lives so vividly that we can see them.'

'I . . . it's like I can see Mei Mei and Honour and Rosie and Pash,' Ayesha says.

'Better be careful or you'll be shipped off to IMH with those words. Speaking of which, we head there tomorrow,' says Jimmy.

'IMH?' says Ayesha.

'The Institute for Mental Health,' says Jimmy, 'to see Vee.'

'Vee? She's still alive?' asks Ayesha.

'Yes. It will take time, but we need to speak with her, she's had a terrible life,' says Jimmy.

'Is there is a caretaker here now?' asks Ayesha.

'Yes, an old Malay woman is here, says her name is Ling Li,' says Jimmy.

Ayesha almost falls to the ground with this news. Ling Li, the woman Isabelle claims rescued her, brought her life.

'Ling Li is here in the house?' asks Ayesha.

'You know her?' asks Jimmy.

'She's responsible for Mei Mei, for how all this started in the first place,' says Ayesha.

'Shall we have a quick word with her?' says Jimmy. 'You must be tired.'

In the small room at the very back of the kitchen house, they see an old woman sitting on the edge of the made-up cot. She has a small shrine and is burning paper effigies and silently saying a prayer and moving the plumes of incense smoke up and over her head in a rhythmic motion.

'Let's leave her, let her be, for now,' says Ayesha.

Chapter Thirty-Five

DETECTIVE AYESHA NUR

1999

Singapore

The Institute for Mental Health is at the far northeastern end of the island. It is a low-level institutional facility surrounded by a barbed wire fence. Manicured gardens create a sense of calm when what is inside the wards is a different reality. The hospital grounds are surrounded by the ubiquitous housing development blocks or HDBs. A brightly coloured playground stands empty in the heat of the day. Ayesha sees a van enter the emergency at the back of the building and watches as patients file out of the van shackled together wearing bright orange jumpsuits.

'The violent offenders are housed at the back of the main buildings, behind the silver-tipped barbed wire over there,' says Jimmy.

'Not Vee, she wouldn't be classified as violent, would she?' asks Ayesha.

Ayesha and Jimmy review the file on Vathaarshi Roy, Vee. The notes state that she was first imprisoned in 1951 and for ten years stayed in Changi Prison until she lost the will to get up off her mat. A sympathetic guard must have reviewed her case and recommended her to Woodlands Hospital, now the officious sounding Institute for Mental Health. It has been over three decades now and Vee has always refused to discuss her case. Her one activity is to attend the adult art therapy programme.

Gathered around a long table, an art therapist works with a group of elderly patients. Another long-term patient looks agitated that Ayesha and Jimmy are in the room. She cups her pointed chin with her stubby fingers and looks from side to side. She chews on the inside of her cheeks, Ayesha notices she has no teeth. An elderly Chinese gentleman joins the long table and takes his time to choose the right shade of pastels. He starts a childlike drawing of the kampong life he must have known growing up before the government-built HDBs transformed the landscape of his Singapore. The man paints a broad-leafed palm tree, fruit trees, open fields, a water buffalo, and a dog.

Ayesha looks down the table and sees the woman they are there to interview. Vee sits all alone. Ayesha sees a copy of *The Straits Times* folded on the table in front of Vee.

'Are you interested in the news?' asks Ayesha.

Vee does not respond. She begins her drawing.

'She draws the same image every day,' says the therapist quietly. 'She won't talk. Has never opened her mouth to utter a phrase.'

Ayesha and Jimmy watch as Vee sketches a dark-skinned woman lying on the ground with her hands above her head, her face turned away from a nurse in a white uniform carrying a wicker shield and bamboo pole. The nurse in the picture is beating the Tamil woman. Vee sighs, and with her downcast eyes and slow-moving hands, beckons Ayesha towards her.

'Nnn,' says Vee.

Ayesha matches her hushed tone to let her know that she understands. Ayesha pulls up a seat and sits with Vee for the remainder of the art session. Jimmy moves a stool closer to where the elderly man continues to draw, when they hear a faint voice coming from Vee.

'My baby, I lost my baby, very late. Same time Rosie was born. I say I have extra milk,' she says.

Ayesha is stunned that she is speaking, but keeps calm and listens. The art therapist stops putting away the art supplies and stands still.

'I still have milk, I fed Rosie when Ma'am Hamilton was sick,' says Vee.

Ayesha feels like she owes Vee a silence. A listening space.

'I fed her and then was blamed for her death. I was beaten and put into jail. Now I live my life here,' says Vee.

'I'm so sorry. Tell me more Vathaarshi,' says Ayesha.

'This woman,' Vee points to a mugshot on page three of *The Straits Times*. It is the photo of Isabelle Goh in London. It is the story the BBC has posted. 'Domestic maid turned international criminal mind' reads the headline.

'This woman, I cared for her and she and everyone else turned on me, betrayed me,' says Vee.

The older patients raise their heads up and the art therapist murmurs how surprised she is to hear Vee speak. Vee looks up at Ayesha, her eyes open wide.

'My life, destroyed, everyone lied,' Vee cries out.

The whole room turns. Ayesha stays seated next to Vee as she lets out a sigh so deep and loud, it could crack open the heart of the earth. Vee reaches for Ayesha's hands.

'I am here, to help you,' says Ayesha.

'No, no you cannot,' says Vee. 'Too dangerous now, see.'

Vee is pointing at the newspaper.

'Who is he?' asks Vee, pointing at Jimmy.

'He's my colleague, hoping to help you,' says Ayesha.

Vee looks away and starts to weep. The other patients start to sob as they pick up on Vee's sadness.

'I've been wanting to talk such a-a long time,' says Vee.

'Well, me and my colleague, we are here to listen, we want to help you,' says Ayesha.

'Why won't anyone believe me?' she starts to stand up.

'Madame Roy, please sit down,' says the art therapist.

'It. Was. Never. Me,' says Vee through her teeth, punctuating her every breath.

'Madame Roy, please, sit down,' says the therapist.

'No. I will not. If you've come all this way to find me, then find who destroyed my life, find Zandstra, find Mei Mei, they ruined everything!' screams Vee.

'I think that's enough visitor time for today,' says the therapist.

'We, we need more time with her,' Ayesha says.

'Not today. As you can see, she has upset the patients,' says the therapist.

The patients grunt and get up from the table. They are disturbed by the noise and move about, clearing the table full of art supplies.

Dusk comes with a low-lying orange sun, then it drops, crashes down exhausted, bringing darkness close. Day shuts down fast in the tropics. Ayesha closes the lid of her laptop and pulls on her running shoes. With a slight hop, she reaches for her water bottle. She's training for the London marathon and aims for a twelve-kilometre run tonight. Running helps her think. She can only run at night here when the temperature and humidity have decreased enough to make it tolerable. She wonders about Vee and the case against her that looked rigged from the beginning. Vee, the woman linked to Mei Mei and Rosie, a plea across history to close the mystery.

The marble floor in the mirrored elevator brings Ayesha quickly down from the eighteenth storey of her serviced apartment and as she raises her hand in salutation to the concierge, she pumps the disinfectant dispenser and rubs the antibacterial gel in between her fingers. The smell is clinical, she can feel the chemicals enter her skin: It stings, just for a moment, but the sting opens and closes a deeper wound in Ayesha that will never heal. She pushes the neon spiral bracelet attached to her key card up above her elbow and winces at the tight pinch that follows.

As she steps out from the air-conditioned hotel lobby, the heat and humidity hit her dead on. The first few blocks, she walks, finds her body's rhythm, and then, with a skip, begins her run, breathing her mantra: *You can do it, Ayesha. You can do it, Ayesha.* Not far from the glamorous Orchard Road condos, trucks roar by carrying Bangladeshi construction workers in the back like chattel. These grown men sit hunched in the back of vehicles sucking on straws dipped into plastic bags of coffee sweetened with condensed milk. Ayesha smells sewage and sulphur, clove cigarettes, and gasoline. She clears her throat. Soon she crosses Scotts Road and heads up towards Newton Circle, passing the outdoor hawker stands, their fluorescent lighting shifting shadows across the night.

She is careful not to lose her footing as she hops around burnt offerings of paper money, Hell banknotes lit to appease the hungry ghosts. The garish colours have faded under the sun, making them look like budget comics. Miniature shrines set up in front of gated residences look childish to her eye. Oranges are grouped around candles burned right here off the road.

It is Ramadan and this Friday night as she passes the Masjid Abdul Hamid, more men are gathered around than usual. She pulls her running shirt away from her chest and adjusts her shorts to appear less obvious about showing so much skin. Cheap brown plastic sandals line the front of the mosque. She watches taxi drivers putting on their prayer caps. A group of taller men wearing long white flowing robes and keffiyeh, speak softly into their Bluetooth gadgets. Younger boys shake hands with their elders then immediately take the same hand and hold it to their own hearts.

Ayesha counts when she runs. She starts with a soft whistle through her teeth and lips, adjusting her breath to match her right heel as it lands on the concrete. She passes the construction sites that are everywhere. Mixed with the call to prayer, she hears faint singing in what sounds like it could be Bangla and smells dhal cooking—a sign that workers are sleeping illegally on site. There is an impressively large sign affixed to the metal fencing around the new underground transit hub. 'FIGHT DENGUE' it reads in alarmingly red font. Enlarged photos of a mosquito, standing water, and a swollen torso warn passers-by of the cruel and painful fever.

Her usual path takes her to the corner of Ardmore Park then a right onto Balmoral and across the intersection of Dunearn and Bukit Timah. Here Balmoral is now called Chancery Lane. She passes the same group of Filipino maids every night, walking pedigreed western dog breeds. There is a dalmatian, a basset hound, and two corgis: their elongated tongues hang low, touching the pavement.

She heads left off Chancery Lane and up onto Mount Rosie Road. Her pace slows and she takes in the shifting geography, the road is slick with green moss and the topography is hilly, winding turns, up and around vast properties. It is so humid, Ayesha feels like she's running in a sauna. Up ahead, there are no street lights and it is heavy jungle. The palm trees are so tall, Ayesha cannot see their tops. Thick trunks of trees with ropes of vegetation tangling their roots reach skyward, giving the jungle a momentum, a feeling of being alive. Ayesha finds herself drawn to this place, the wide-open field, an uncommon site in Singapore, giving her eyes a chance to roam and rest, there it is: 24 Mount Rosie Road. She stops and sees the same woman she saw before lighting lamps in the garden.

'Hello?' asks Ayesha. 'Hello?'

'Yes?' answers the woman.

The woman walks towards the gates. She is holding a broom.

'I . . . I am looking for . . .' begins Ayesha.

'Nobody here, Ma'am, no one live her for long time,' says the woman.

'I'm looking for Ling Li,' says Ayesha.

The woman is silent and comes closer to the gate.

'That is me,' she says. 'No one ever is looking for me.'

'Can I talk with you?' asks Ayesha.

'Please, come in,' says Ling Li.

Ayesha is guided up the lane and towards the kitchen house. They sit across from one another on plastic stools.

'I have been following the case of Isabelle, Isabelle Goh,' says Ayesha.

'Mei Mei,' says Ling Li.

'What do you make of all this?' asks Ayesha.

'Too much imagination, lah,' says Ling Li.

'How do you mean?' asks Ayesha.

'She was always curious, even as a girl, a small girl, all the time, never let anything just be,' says Ling Li. 'Maybe because she always wondered, always wonder who her real family was, you know? I mean I tried, but I also no family, so did my best.'

'I am here investigating the case. Vee, and all the reasons why someone might want to kill Mei Mei,' says Ayesha.

'Yes, I know,' says Ling Li. 'You won't find much. I'm just being real, truthful. That time was bad, so different now. Now the world much bigger, back then it was small. Mei Mei knew it was big and tried to throw herself at the whole world, but the rest of us, we all took a small piece of what could be ours. We should have just listened to the feng shui master, to save our money, worship the ancestors.'

'Thank you, Ling Li, you have been very helpful, please let me know if you have anything more to share,' says Ayesha.

'What about Rosie, have you found her?' asks Ling Li.

'Not yet,' says Ayesha.

'Please tell me when you have, I always wondered, what she would look like, you know . . . who her father was,' says Ling Li.

'Do you? Do you know who her father . . . who is Rosie's father?' asks Ayesha.

'Best keep it a mystery,' says Ling Li.

Ayesha wants to stay and talk, but Ling Li ushers her back down the road. Ayesha waves goodbye and makes her way back down towards the main intersection but is alarmed to see a thick green and brown python in the open drain. She loses her balance and almost falls. She feels clammy and wants to sit down. Her head aches and in this heat, she feels a chill, a metallic taste in her mouth that makes her want to spit. She grasps out towards the road and falls sideways into a lacey pine. Ayesha lurches forward and falls on her knees.

Ayesha wakes up in her serviced apartment, shaking and cold, a fever holds her in its grip. She hallucinates about the house on 24 Mount Rosie Road and sees birds, all kinds of birds, feeding at the swimming pool. Her bed feels hard and she watches as exotic birds congregate all around her on the bed. She can't sleep and wakes up in a sweat and fear sets into her gut. She is aching everywhere and can't understand what is wrong. She has never felt so ill, she can't even reach for the water bottle. Later in the early evening, there is a knock on her door and Jimmy stands beside her, holding her wrist and feeling her forehead. She is delirious, she can't even sit up.

Chapter Thirty-Six

ISABELLE GOH

1999

London

'I'm going blind. It is terrifying. I can't see out of my left eye and my right eye is clouded. I can't make sense . . . pocket of my robe . . . Detective, are you there?'

'Mei Mei, it's me. I'm here,' says Honour.

'You?' I ask.

'Yes, it's me, Honour.'

I'm trapped. My mouth is suddenly dry and I can smell my own breath. It smells like fear.

'Do you know what going blind feels like?' I ask.

'No,' says Honour.

'It's like facing a void of endless space . . . and I'm afraid,' I say.

'You? Afraid?' says Honour.

'Leave me, leave me alone,' I say.

'You will be sorry you never said what you've always wanted,' she says.

I am the weaker of the two of us. I am prey. I am the hornbill flapping in the corner of the box.

'Why make this harder than it needs to be,' I say.

'It doesn't need to be hard,' says Honour. 'Just tell me, tell me where she is. Where is Rosie?'

'I don't know,' I reply. 'Honestly.'

'I know Pash was helping you pay to keep her safe,' says Honour.

'Well, I should hope so, wouldn't want any secrets to come between a happily married couple.'

'We've been separated for two years,' says Honour.

'Oh?' I say. 'What brought that on?'

'What would you care?' asks Honour.

'I know he came to tell me . . .' An acute attack of pain rooted in the inside of my brain makes me gasp in pain. 'You . . . you've done enough, just let me be.'

'Come now, Mei Mei, don't end it like this, leave the envy, the resentment aside,' says Honour.

'Easy for you to say,' I say.

'You and I both know it was hell at the end with Zandstra,' says Honour.

'It was hell at the beginning, middle, *and* end,' I say.

'Come on, we had some fun, you had the most wonderful imagination,' says Honour.

'Ah yes, but it was responsible for all my pain, all of it,' I tell her. 'Look where I've landed, all because I imagined I deserved more.'

'Two old birds,' says Honour.

I have another attack of acute pain and Honour responds by holding my hands and stroking my face.

'What does it matter after all? I've had so many enemies,' I say. 'I do wish it had worked out differently. You were so lucky to get Pash, he really is a decent man. The only one I ever knew.'

'Don't go there, Mei Mei,' says Honour.

'I can't last much longer, it's the end. You know, the moment I leave, they will find Rosie, that's the way it has to be,' I tell her. 'Tell me something, tell me how Zandstra died.'

'Don't you remember?' Honour asks.

'I want to remember it again,' I say.

'It was when you came back after securing Rosie's safety, and Vee was taken. It was chaos. Tessa and Angus were gone. I was lost, I had nothing to lose. Zandstra had started drinking earlier than normal. We could tell by the smell on his breath that he had already had much to drink in Sir's study. He'd been in there most of the day, alone. You remember, don't you?' says Honour.

'Tell me again,' I say to Honour.

I can sense another person enter the room and hear the nurse, the one called Rory, speak softly to Honour. I close my eyes and imagine us there at the great house—Pash, Honour, and me—waiting under the veranda to execute our plan. I sense Honour is near my IV pole, she is opening another bag of some sort of solution.

'I walked with him along the jungle path to Malcolm Road and Pash followed behind, remember? You raced ahead and waited inside the Zandstras' home, you knew where all the keys were. Once we got inside his house, he pushed me inside the bathroom, and he . . . he showed me his . . . he smoothed it down with cream and . . . the window was open behind him so I jumped through it and ran back to where you and Pash had locked the bathroom door shut from the outside, locking Zandstra inside,' says Honour.

'Yes, I remember,' I say. I am feeling very cold and light-headed, my breathing is slowing down.

'You had soaked the towels with whiskey. I carried them to the bathroom window from the outside and shoved them inside the bathroom and then you struck the match. You did it. It wasn't the inferno that we had hoped, but he did scream and he . . . he suffocated from the smoke. You remember this, you've got to remember this,' says Honour.

'God, we were good, how did we—' I begin to ask as another attack of pain makes me fold over.

'We had no choice but to keep Rosie safe. Won't be long now, Mei Mei. You will feel no pain.'

I feel like I'm falling, falling, and as I fall, I see Ayesha, the woman who has been trying to put together my story, I reach for her wrist.

Chapter Thirty-Seven

DETECTIVE AYESHA NUR

1999

Singapore

In the febrile stages of her fever, Ayesha drifts through layers of shimmering light. Her breathing is shallow. She falls deeper and deeper into a split in the earth, where her breath is pressed into her upper chest. She feels a pronounced ache around her heart when she feels someone grab her wrist. It is a shock and she looks at who has such a firm grip on her. Ayesha moves her arms in front of her face, grasping for open space and air. She is in and out of consciousness, fighting this biphasic fever for two days.

'Get out, get out of here!' says a voice.

Ayesha tries to make sense of the voice. It sounds like Mei Mei's voice. But is it real or imagined?

'Where am I?' asks Ayesha into the abyss.

'With me. No one wants to be here, get out, get better, live!' says the voice. It is Mei Mei's voice. 'Thank you for trying,' she says.

Ayesha tries to respond, but no words come. When Ayesha wakes, she uses all her strength to sit up. Jimmy is there holding her hand.

'How are you feeling? You've been very sick,' he says.

'Exhausted,' she says.

'It's all over,' he says. 'Isabelle Goh died last night.'

Ayesha knows now that it was Mei Mei she saw in her fever dream. Ayesha is at once relieved and devastated to learn that Isabelle is dead. All this work. What will come of it? Will Ayesha ever find Rosie?

'We still need to find Rosie, and the person who tried to end Mei Mei's life.'

'Never mind that, it is not important, your health is the most important thing now, please, rest,' says Jimmy. 'You will be interested to know that Honour, Dr Honour Hamilton, was with Mei Mei when she died,' says Jimmy.

'Honour and Mei Mei, just as it should be,' says Ayesha.

'And, you're going to be interested in this. They found a deed to a property in Singapore in the pocket of her robe,' says Jimmy.

'I don't understand,' says Ayesha.

'Mei Mei left property to Rosie,' says Jimmy.

'What property,' I ask.

'Rest, when you are better, we have work to do, we need to find Rosie. For now, rest,' says Jimmy.

Ayesha is discharged from Mount Elizabeth Hospital by the familiar sound of the palm of a doctor's hand sweeping purposefully across a prescription pad. The last time she remembered this sound was the day she was cleared to leave the hospital after her severe depression. For days afterwards, Ayesha could hear faraway sounds as if they were amplified right beside her. When Zoe cried, Ayesha would hide under her own blankets, the noise too pronounced for her to respond accurately. This was a dark time when thankfully her own mother helped to adjust Ayesha to her new normal.

'You are lucky to be alive,' says the doctor. 'You were a very sick lady. Dengue and septic shock. You will be all right, but you will need at least a month's rest. Do you have somewhere to stay in Singapore? I do not advise travel.'

'You stay with me and recover,' says Jimmy.

'I'll be in the way of your family,' I say.

'No, please. Come on it's old-time detective work. You and me, we can do this,' says Jimmy.

Ayesha's phone rings.

'Detective Nur?' says Christian Gaul.

'Speaking,' says Ayesha.

'Interpol sees no further reason to examine Isabelle Goh now that she is deceased. We've closed the file. The funds are no longer available to pursue this case. I'm sure you are aware of the costs involved in an international criminal case,' says Gaul.

'I'm sure I do. Thank you, Inspector,' says Ayesha.

'Madame, before I go, thank you, thank you for your work. One of your requests from us came up with a positive address. We have located a Maria Rosamund Lee, *née* Roy, she has an office in the Bank of China building. Sounds like an impressive person.'

'Rosie? Really? Oh my. Thank you,' Ayesha responds.

Ayesha stands up and immediately buckles back down into the clinic chair.

'You okay?' asks Jimmy.

'That was Interpol. We're off the case, officially off, and . . . they have a lead on Rosie,' says Ayesha.

'Rosie? That's amazing,' says Jimmy.

'What do we do now?' says Ayesha.

'We pursue the case on our own. What else are you going to do for four weeks? The visitor's visa has been extended and you have to stay and rest,' says Jimmy.

'Too much all at once. Mei Mei is dead, and Rosie is found, I can't believe it. Interpol came through for us in the end. They gave us a contact for Rosie,' says Ayesha.

'Where to first, then? IMH again or the hunt for Rosie?' asks Jimmy.

'IMH, I want to be the one to tell Vee that Mei Mei is dead,' says Ayesha.

Ayesha and Jimmy head to IMH to interview Vee again. Vee stands in the art therapy room waiting for them.

'I heard you were unwell, you must take good care,' says Vee and envelops Ayesha in a warm embrace.

'I'm going to be all right. We have news,' says Ayesha.

'Tell me!' says Vee.

'Mei Mei, she's dead,' says Ayesha.

Vee gasps and closes her eyes. It is also the first time Ayesha has really processed it and it hits her, more than she had thought, the woman, the case, all gone. Vee loses her balance and reaches for a chair.

'This is not how I thought my life would be, that a young girl could ruin my life, but, in the end, who would ever have guessed . . . I'm the one still alive,' says Vee.

'And . . . we have a lead on where Rosie is,' says Jimmy.

'Rosie!' shouts Vee. 'She's here, I knew it.'

'She is indeed,' says Ayesha. 'At least the address we have for her is here in Singapore. And one more thing.'

'Yes?' asks Vee.

'Ling Li, she's in the house. She never left,' says Ayesha.

Vee closes her eyes and breathes in slowly.

'We have both been prisoners,' says Vee.

'One way to think of it,' says Jimmy.

'But why, why you even care, Ms Ayesha, why you care so much?' asks Vee.

'I care because that's my job,' says Ayesha.

Vee sighs and looks past Ayesha.

'You're a good person,' says Vee.

'Nothing is ever easy,' says Ayesha. 'You deserve freedom now.'

'You know, I don't know I even know what that would be like, freedom, I will be ready someday,' says Vee. 'I've been in these walls for so long. You know, I only had two visitors in all these years.'

'Who? Who came to visit you?' asks Ayesha.

'Honour, Miss. Honour Hamilton and my nephew, Pash,' says Vee. 'They came to tell me they were married.'

'Were you happy? To know they were married?' asks Ayesha.

'I never got to see them. The guards never let me see them, just passed the message,' Vee responds.

'Oh, I'm so sorry,' says Ayesha.

'Can't be helped,' says Vee. 'Detective, tell me, you also seem lost, looking to be found. Excuse me for saying. You lost someone too?'

'Yes, myself. I almost lost myself,' says Ayesha.

Chapter Thirty-Eight

ROSIE

1999

Singapore

On Saturdays, Maria Rosamund Lee, known to her friends and colleagues as Rosie, wanders the cool halls of the Asian Civilizations Museum. She's turned to memorizing the ancient trade routes outlined on the walls. She sees images of the Singapore river serving as an entrepôt for Chinese junks, Buginese schooners, and Arab dhows bringing tradesmen, boats, spices, and prayers. She imagines the subtle change in the direction of the winds across the Strait this time of the year when the moon's pull is strong and for a day or two, the air is dry like the desert. There are no clouds of haze or humidity; these are the winds of change when for a moment all is well in the world.

She continues reading about the young Prince from Palembang, now South Sumatra, who while hunting in the area in the sixteenth century saw what he thought was a lion and called this place 'Singa Pura' or Lion City. Hundreds of years of monsoon winds later, traders and travellers have come to this place on disparate winds, growing empires and preventing the advance of their enemies. Now it seems to Rosie the winds are all messed up and keep crashing into each other. Strange winds blow.

A new exhibition on Singaporean architecture is open. One wall showcases photographs of the colonial homes of the British administration known as black and whites. Rosie hears a docent announce a tour is about to begin and she tags along at the back of the group. The tour guide explains that many of these old homes now house galleries and upscale restaurants. Rosie wonders what it would have been like to have lived in one of these estates. The idea intrigues her and she lingers at one photograph while the tour moves on through the exhibit. It is an image of a family gathered around the front of a black and white.

She leans in closer and sees a baby cradled in the arms of a large Tamil woman. An Asian girl stands with her hand holding onto the baby's gown, possessively. It looks like a christening shot. An elderly Caucasian woman stands beside a well-dressed gentleman and a woman who looks very pale. Rosie is intrigued by the face of a young woman who stands slightly apart from the group. She has long brown hair and an air of aloofness as if she really didn't want to be in the photograph. There is a Malay man, a Chinese man, and a tall, handsome young Indian man. The letters at the bottom in yellowed typeface form the names of Angus Hamilton, Tessa Hamilton, Honour Hamilton, Rosamund Hamilton, and Faith Arundel Ducharmes. The staff have no names. The date given is 1950. Rosie peers into the photograph trying to decipher who these people are. She feels connected to this image somehow. Rosie sees an address underneath the photograph. 24 Mount Rosie Road.

Rosie continues looking at more photographs of these houses, and learns how the black and whites were used for shooting parties, how many of the grander homes were used as Japanese war bases, where some were used to keep comfort women. Then the post-war wave of developers demolished many of them to make way for modern high-rises to house Singaporean families.

She sees another enlarged photo of a house on Malcolm Road. A large, burly Caucasian man stands on the front steps beside a petite woman with closely shorn hair. Under the photo is typed a Dutch name: Zandstra. The very last photo in the exhibit is of three children. Two girls and one boy stand in front of a Christmas tree. The scene is juxtaposed with tropical foliage in the background. She looks closely and sees the faces of three young children, she can see they are the same three children from the photograph of the christening party at the house on Mount Rosie Road.

In a particular light, at a certain angle, Rosie's complexion has been described as alabaster, white and smooth and even more pronounced against her shoulder-length, black, wavy hair. Her high cheekbones and long face seem out of place with her crescent-shaped black eyes. Her European DNA gives her height, and her Asian eyes have always been described as exotic. Rosie knows she is half Asian—the other half she has never known. All she has been told is that a rich uncle, connected to the church, had paid for her education, but other than that, her personal history is a mystery.

She steps out of the darkness of the museum and into the midday sun where she is temporarily blinded. From the front of the museum, the view of the city is particularly impressive. The Cavanagh Bridge frames the evolution of this city from low-level shophouses one hundred years ago to the houses of finance looming high into the skyline. She is reminded of her reality. Rosie works at the very top of the tallest glass tower. The trade is no longer in silk damasks but in oil, steel, and rare metals. For all the money she has made, she is miserable. She has lost her marriage of twenty-five years, and is close to losing her job.

It was a successful marriage until her husband expanded his interests into younger women. With the move to Singapore for her job last year, she confronted him with his dalliances. David caved and Rosie didn't have the energy to fight. So, here she finds herself middle-aged and alone. From her office tower, she finds time to explore certain landmarks and get a sense of the city.

Rosie has been having dreams lately, vivid dreams that she's not sure how to explain: a young girl is handed around a circle of smiling faces. She aches to share them with someone but hasn't met anyone yet she could disclose this to, and Rosie can't shake the feeling of being there in this circle of smiles. And just now, that photograph in the exhibition, how is it that she feels a deep connection to it?

In the middle of the heat of the day, she walks towards Victoria Hall and to the open space of the padang. She hasn't gone more than five hundred metres when she turns and looks back towards the city, this city where the currents and winds have shifted her life. Across the padang, she sees the cathedral spires. The heat bears down on her as she walks towards them, entering under the whitewashed roof and is calmed by the beauty of the space.

Sky blue paint sets off three panels of floor-to-ceiling stained glass windows behind the altar. Rosie reads the names on the marble slabs that cover the walls: names of children and men and women, too young to die. She reaches out and fingers the letters of a tablet erected on a pillar. Engraved in a deep font, are the names of two people who died within days of each other. It's as if she can feel the pain of loss in the spaces in between the letters.

Tessa Hamilton, born April 15, 1920,
in Georgetown, British Malaya. Died December 16, 1950, in Singapore.
Loving wife to Angus Hamilton. Mother to baby Rosie.

Angus Hamilton born 1898
in Tisbury, Wiltshire, England. Died December 13, 1950, in Singapore
Loving husband to Tessa Hamilton. Father to baby Rosie.

Rosie stops and makes the connection. These are the same people from the photograph in the museum.

It is too much loss at once. Rosie stumbles through the east doors and past the National Museum and up the outdoor escalators built into the hillside up to Fort Canning Park. She walks through the foreigners' cemetery and sees the familiar words of grief, not in English but in German and Russian. Inside the brick walls of the English cemetery, the dead are separated by their denomination: the Catholics on the left and Protestants on the right. Dark green tropical vines cover many of the plaques on the brick. Many are so damaged from the elements that the words and dates are illegible, making her feel time rushing past, leaving vast emptiness.

Rosie steps out of the elevator onto the thirty-fourth floor of her office tower and into the waiting area. She is drenched from the afternoon she has spent wandering from the Asian Civilizations Museum to the Fort Canning tombstones. Ayesha and Jimmy are sitting in the bright orange chairs. They rise when she walks in.

'Maria Rosamund Lee?' asks Ayesha.

'It's Rosie, just Rosie. Can I help you?' says Rosie. She looks around for the receptionist. No one is at the front desk.

'This is Detective Ibrahim from the Singapore Police Force and I am Detective Nur from the London Metropolitan Police,' says Ayesha.

'Oh, God! What has happened?' asks Rosie.

'Please don't be alarmed, may we sit somewhere privately?' asks Jimmy.

'Of course, this way,' says Rosie.

'We have been waiting to meet you for a long time,' says Ayesha.

'We hope you can make time to meet, there is considerable information to share with you,' says Jimmy.

'Yes, of course,' says Rosie.

Rosie walks down the hallway, past empty offices, all with extensive views of the Singapore river: the old colonial buildings now the Asian Civilizations Museum, the Victoria Theatre, the National Gallery, the Fullerton hotel, the padang, and St Andrew's cathedral. As they walk down the hall, Jimmy and Ayesha make small talk.

'Impressive office space,' says Jimmy.

'Thank you,' says Rosie.

'How long have you worked here?' asks Ayesha.

'In Singapore?' asks Rosie.

'Yes,' says Jimmy.

'Just over a year,' says Rosie.

'Settled in then?' asks Jimmy.

'More or less,' says Rosie. 'In here, please take a seat. Would you excuse me a moment to freshen up?'

Rosie leaves the board room and heads to the washroom connected to her corner office. She is unusually flustered and dehydrated. 'Please, not David,' she says to herself in the mirror. 'Slow down.' She dries the small of her back with the hand towels. *Who are these people and what could they want?* She leads a highly organized life and people rarely get on her calendar without her knowing. She takes a few deep breaths to compose herself and forces a smile. Her reflection shows an exhausted version of herself. She pinches her cheeks as she heads back to the conference room and the waiting police officers.

'Have you been offered a drink?' asks Rosie. 'I'm not sure where the receptionist is.'

'Thank you. All good. We are here to share some news with you,' begins Jimmy.

Rosie doesn't know what to do with her hands so she slips them under her legs, holding herself still. Her teeth start to chatter.

'Is it David? Tell me it's not David,' she says.

'No. Not your husband David.'

'Ex-husband,' corrects Rosie.

'Right. Ms Lee, you have been left a piece of property, an inheritance from a woman, a woman named, Isabelle . . .'

'Come again? An inheritance?' says Rosie.

'Yes,' says Steve.

'But I am an orphan, I never knew my parents,' says Rosie. 'I don't know anyone who could possibly . . .'

'A woman, named Isabelle Goh, has left you the deed to property here in Singapore,' says Ayesha.

'You must be mistaken,' says Rosie.

'You would have known her as Mei Mei,' says Ayesha.

'Mei Mei? No, I don't know anyone, you must have the wrong person, so sorry,' says Rosie.

'You will be contacted by her lawyers as well as the man who was your formal guardian, he is based in London. We want you to know that,' says Jimmy.

Rosie is stunned. She knew a man had financially supported her, but now a woman, an inheritance? She doesn't know what to do next except cry.

'How?' she manages through her tears. 'I mean, I knew someone was paying for my school fees, but I never . . . who is she, was she?'

'It's a very long story and one that you will learn in your own time, when you are ready,' says Jimmy.

'Come on, tell me more,' says Rosie. 'You can't come all this way. Please, give me more, more information about my own life.'

'What we know Rosie is that this woman who has passed, she was the domestic maid at the house where you were born. It is a lot, I know. She worked for a couple named the Hamiltons, Angus and Tessa and their niece, Honour,' says Ayesha.

Rosie can't believe what she is hearing . . . the names from the exhibit, from the cathedral.

'There is more, much more, but we can leave the story for you to find out on your own at your own pace,' says Ayesha. 'You let us know when you want to see the property.'

'My mother, who was my mother?' asks Rosie.

'Her name was Tessa Hamilton,' says Jimmy.

'And my father, who . . . any idea who my father was?' she asks.

'Uncertain, perhaps a business partner of your mother's husband,' says Jimmy.

Rosie is quiet. She looks out at the expansive view of Singapore.

'I always hoped that I would learn about my past, but an inheritance is a surprise,' she says turning to them. 'This is really all too much.' As she dries her tears, she realizes she is laughing. Crying and laughing at the same time.

'We completely understand,' says Ayesha.

'Thank you, detectives. I have had a big change in my life and now this, it is overwhelming, all of this.' She sighs. 'Singapore. Singapore has made a mark already, I mean . . . I certainly would never have known my connection was to this place. Let's say we go now, can we see the property now?'

'Absolutely,' say Ayesha and Jimmy at the same time.

The three of them drive from the Bank of China building through the city and over to the shophouses around Emerald Hill. The same roads Mei Mei and Honour took more than fifty years ago on a rickshaw to find counsel from the feng shui master. The elegant mix of European and Chinese baroque architecture winding through the streets is a direct contrast to the sky-high corporate towers where Rosie spends most of her days. Here, each façade of the shophouses is completely different one from another. Some are painted in bright colours: purple or blue.

'I never knew you could live here,' says Rosie.

'It's just up here on Saunders Road, No, 2 Saunders Road,' says Jimmy.

They park the police car and walk up towards the corner property.

The shophouse extends far down an entire block. It is painted a soft yellow. A flowering jacaranda tree extends its branches across the front, shedding purple blossoms across the front steps. There is a private forecourt and on the first-floor windows, tiles in soft pastels of pink, blue, green, and yellow feature birds and flowers.

'Let's see if someone is there, to let you in,' says Ayesha.

'Are you sure we can do this?' asks Rosie.

'Yes, we contacted the property manager, they are around. This is yours now,' says Jimmy.

'Did Mei Mei ever live here?' asks Rosie.

'Mei Mei might have come here as a girl, this was an area where a renowned feng shui master worked, this property was his base, where he welcomed all his clients,' says Jimmy.

A woman steps out of the shophouse.

'You must be Maria Lee,' says the property manager.

'Yes,' says Rosie quietly.

'Welcome to your new home!' says the woman.

Ayesha, Jimmy, and Rosie look up at the house and admire the Chinese rococo design, featuring ornamentations of birds, animals, and flowers. Ayesha looks closely and is struck to see a tiger and a phoenix. The two animals are interlocked like a dancing duo. Ayesha stands back further from the shophouse and looks up at the second storey. She can make out a hornbill and a koel, frangipani and mangosteen. Ayesha begins to understand now, she begins to understand how much Mei Mei loved Rosie and that these images and this house are Rosie's to uncover.

'Come on, let's go in,' says Jimmy.

Ayesha places her arm on Rosie's shoulder.

'It's all yours,' says Ayesha.

As they walk to the centre of the house, they are startled to see a frangipani tree growing in the middle of the space. A large air well opens directly to the sky and floods the shophouse with light. Tiles featuring a tiger and a phoenix in an elaborate dance are featured throughout the space.

'Oh my, such a beautiful place!' says Rosie.

'Yours to discover,' says Ayesha. 'We'll leave you here, wishing you all the best.'

'Thank you,' says Rosie.

Chapter Thirty-Nine

DETECTIVE AYESHA NUR

January 2000

Singapore

Before Ayesha leaves Singapore, she searches for time on her own to make sense of all she has experienced, to process what she has learned. She has worked on her first international case that on the surface looked like a gang assassination but which ballooned into a family saga, where she met a wanted criminal, a Bishop, a leading psychiatrist, and found the woman they had been protecting all these years.

Ayesha needs to settle her mind and to prepare to return home, to Zoe, to life as a mother and daughter and back to another case. Ayesha hears of the Thaipusam festival where devotees carry their debts, their burdens asking for help from Lord Murugan, the vanquisher of evil. She is curious about this. She is attracted to the idea of being part of a human experience where she can give over her pain, her suffering, a true manifestation, a redemptive quest for healing.

She hears the low voices first and then the movement of robes, of saris, of feet against the pavement. As she joins the pull of men and women, many wearing robes the colour of turmeric, she is folded into the crowd, ushered into the procession. She is overwhelmed by the heat, the press of humanity.

In the parade, her spirits are awakened enough for her to think about Zoe, about her own depression. She has a vision that she is holding hands with her beautiful Zoe. The two of them float in the air like a two-headed sycamore seed spiralling down. As they dance on the air, moving down, down to the soil, they hold each other with their eyes a deep, deep, dark brown—a love so rich and powerful that Ayesha knows this depression does not have a grip on her, that her capacity for love has not been stunted and that she can continue on, strong, knowing that her suffering has opened up a great beauty and joy that she now knows exists. The parade ends with the streets and temple awash with milk, with exhausted, pierced bodies, with spirits lifted high, and with blessings for families for a future of salvation and peace.

At Changi airport, Ayesha stands in line to board the plane back to London. She feels changed. Singapore has made her determined to excel in her work. She feels this experience has reconstructed her into a better person, filled her with a desire to be a better mother. But these uplifting thoughts come crashing down when Ayesha recognizes the hunched shoulders of Charlie Xiao ahead of her in line. Charlie is around twenty people ahead of her in the boarding queue. She freezes, sensing that being close to this man is an immediate danger. Within seconds, she is in fight mode. She turns and falls further and further back in the line, pulling her baseball cap low over her eyes. She watches him from this distance. He is pulling a steel carry on case. He looks impatient. Her viewpoint is expanded now that she is further down the line and she sees another familiar person—it is that nurse, the one from the A & E, Rory, the one who worked with Honour. Ayesha is torn. She needs to get on this plane but for the entirety of the flight she needs to be invisible. She sends Steve a text. `Charlie. Charlie is on the same plane and the nurse, with the tattoos.` Next, Ayesha sends Jimmy a text. `Jimmy, Keep Rosie safe.`

Chapter Forty

ISABELLE GOH

1999

London

12 November

I park my silver Mercedes in front of my St James's Place apartment and reapply more of my coral-coloured lipstick. I am waiting for Pash. He says he has news. I am also ready to confess to him all my failings. The car is still running when Pash walks up to my car window. It is a cold, foggy grey night. He knocks on the glass and I open the car door for him. He gets in.

'It's been so long Mei Mei, how are you? You been well?' he asks rubbing his hands together.

He looks good. An attractive man. The young boy has turned into the man he was supposed to be. Assured and kind.

'Our project, Miss Rosie, is still doing well,' he says.

'Any news?' I ask him. 'Have you found her?'

'They've found an address for her in . . . Singapore,' he says.

'Imagine, she's found her way home,' I say.

'You've done a good thing, Mei Mei, I mean we all did what we could,' says Pash.

'What about Honour, where is she?' I ask.

'You know where she is. She's still at Charing Cross. Psychiatry. Ready to retire soon,' he says. 'We've separated.'

'Oh, that's a shock,' I say.

'Not really, I'm leaving everything it seems,' he says.

'How do you mean?' I ask.

'I'm leaving,' he says.

'What? You're leaving London?' I ask.

'No, the church,' he says.

'God? What? Really?' I say.

'I'm ceasing my duties, resigning from my position tomorrow afternoon,' says Pash.

'What? You can do that?' I ask.

'With difficulty,' says Pash.

'But why?' I ask.

'I can't hear the beauty any more. People always want something from me, as if I can top up their good deeds with God. I am only going through the motions,' says Pash. 'I'm done, I've had enough meaning making.'

'This is the right thing for you,' I say.

'It is,' he agrees.

'Good night, Pash,' I say.

'Good bye, Mei Mei,' says Pash.

How does one understand a life, Detective? I knew my time was coming and I was ready to make a change. Pash leaves the warmth of the car and I look at the deed of the property one more time. This is my gift for Rosie. She will be found and no matter what happens to me, she will be fine. Everything will be fine.

When my car door is yanked open behind me, I am surprised to see Honour get in, but then I know. I sense a vastness, like a damp cave, the nearness of death like a chasm is falling in front of me. As the gun is wedged against my temple, I know what my heart wants. It wants Rosie. Always Rosie.

'I've been forced to do this,' says Honour.

She holds the gun to my head.

'Do what?' I ask her.

'Pash would never do it,' says Honour. 'Get rid of you. You, you always had to get in the way. The way of us,' says Honour.

'I don't . . .' I say.

'You're a liability now. Pash is on to bigger things,' she says.

'You don't know what you're doing,' I tell her.

With her releasing the trigger, imaginary rope bridges tumble down, broken ladders smash and crack against the rocky shales on the shores of my soul. Honour shoots the gun five times. She never expected me to live, but I came through, Detective, just long enough to know that Rosie has been found. Thank you.

Detective Ayesha Nur is back in London from the investigation in Singapore. She is walking her daughter to school. Zoe is telling her about her new choir teacher. Ayesha is holding her daughter's hand. There is a fresh chill in the air. Ayesha takes a deep breath and registers this new feeling of calm. She is satisfied enough with the case to think about a future, a future with Zoe where they are both happy, where she can embrace being a mother, a better mother to this young girl.

Passing by a parked Mercedes SUV, Ayesha senses danger when she notices the passenger window on the far side has been smashed in. Ayesha doesn't draw attention to what she knows is inside. She bends towards Zoe and tells her that she can go on her own from here. Zoe embraces Ayesha and walks down the street towards her school. Ayesha waves back, knowing that their lives are about to change. Inside the vehicle, Ayesha finds two women shot to death. The neck of one woman is angled and her mouth hangs open to reveal a row of gold teeth. Ayesha inhales and smells the medicinal scent of tiger balm and closes her eyes. 'Mariflores,' says Ayesha to herself. Ayesha's next case has just begun.

Epilogue

I can finally imagine my piece of Heaven, Detective. It is beautiful.

A vast wilderness offers itself to my imagination. The foliage here is forever changing. Green shoots unfurl at every moment, and thick vines lift and carry us up to the heights we are meant to climb. We all know who we are here and carry it in our hearts. Here I can be curious and big and open. I navigate my way through this new earth, discovering colours and textures, smells and tastes I have never experienced. I follow an unlit path that leads deep into the jungle. The closer I come to this dense vegetation, the sky opens up and I feel the ocean calm around me as a ribbon of silt reflects a heaven full of stars.

When I look back and see myself as a young girl at the house on Mount Rosie Road, with Ling Li, Vee, Honour, and Rosie, I see a soul trying to make sense of her world, just like Maria. This is true of me even after being the dutiful girl, after serving others, until swallowing the ugliness of the human heart exposes in me a desire and an attraction to darkness that is so dangerous that even the angels wake up and take notice and look around for their beloved.

Here, in my imagination, I belong, and I am loved. In these bright pages of the end, my heart finds what it wants. We are all together. Me and Rosie and Honour and Maria. The four of us are angels at the four corners of a bed, singing notes into the morning sky. I do not seek retribution but peace, belonging, and Rosie, always Rosie.

For this moment, I will wait, here in the underside of the world.

Acknowledgements

The first book I turned to at the beginning of the pandemic was a book on faith and art by Madeleine L'Engle. From her book, I learned that we cannot create until we acknowledge our own createdness. It is truly a global co-creation to bring this book to readers. Special thanks to my publisher, Nora Nazerene Abu Bakar, for giving the story of Mei Mei, Honour, and Pash a home with Penguin Random House SEA. Thank you to my editors Thatchaayanie Renganathan and Surina Jain for making my manuscript the best it could be. I am grateful for the collaborative design work of Adviata Vats, Divya Gaur, and Swastika Biswas for the beautiful book cover art. Thanks also to Almira Ebio Manduriao and the marketing and publicity team at PRH SEA.

To my teachers, thank you for igniting in me a love of story. To Ms Caulfield, my grade eight English teacher at the Jakarta International School, thank you for turning me into a forever reader. To Claire Keegan, thank you for your brilliant teaching as part of the Asia Creative Writing Programme in Singapore. Thanks to Anna Davis and the Curtis Brown Creative online writing programme team. In Vancouver, thank you to Kevin Chong, Wayde Compton, and Janet Fretter for your mentorship through all things literary. In Toronto, thank you to Thea Lim and Amy Stuart from Flying Books, and to Patricia Westerhof for your encouraging Zoom writing sessions.

To my fellow writing students in Vancouver at The SFU Writer's Studio 2014; Tom Hunter, Jeremy Bisley, Shell Johnson,

Deanna Wigmore, Sheila Galati, Amy Vaughan, Helen Polychronopos, and Tamara Letkeman. Thank you for reading the first drafts of this book.

To my friends in Vancouver, thank you to Elizabeth Moxham, Brenda Campbell, Rosa Flinton-Brown, and Siobhan McLachlan for your encouragement. To Rajha Ghazi Al-Hashmi, shukran, you always know what to read next. To my bosom buddy Rosanne Kang Jovanovski in Los Angeles, thank you, your artistic genius is astounding. In London, thank you to Visha Yogeswaran who encouraged me to dream big. To Cecile Collineau in Jakarta, thank you for telling me to keep writing. To Jessica Purchase in Singapore, thank you for the walks around Mount Rosie Road where the seeds of this novel started. To Singapore based writers Tracey Morton and Kehinde Fadipe, thank you for leading the way. To Dawn Farnham in Australia, thank you for inspiring me to write about Singapore and Maria Hertogh. To Simon Rowe, in Japan, a fellow PRH SEA writer, thank you so much for your generosity.

Special thanks to my parents Dr Jon Scott and Carolyn Scott for encouraging my writing, starting with a no TV household and reems of snail mail correspondence over many decades. Thanks to my brother, Matt Scott, and sister-in-law, Sandra Seaborn, for their support of my writing.

This book is for my husband and the people we made.

I wrote this novel in loving memory of my first friend, Louisa Wawn.

My final thanks is to the writer Jean Rhys who helped me understand our efforts as writers help create more and more art. She said the following: 'All of writing is a huge lake. There are great rivers that feed the lake like Tolstoy and Dostoyevsky. And there are trickles like Jean Rhys. All that matters is feeding the lake. I don't matter. The lake matters. You must keep feeding the lake.'